I0649550

VAYU NAIDU is a novelist and performance storyteller of the oral traditions. Her doctoral work brought out the transposition of cultural and performance nuances through re-imaginings of Indian epics and world myths in English. Her post-doctoral research examined the role of stories and storytelling as a bridge in multilingual contexts, such as education, prisons, immigration and domestic violence. She is now Research Associate in the Department of the Languages and Cultures of South Asia at SOAS University of London.

Arts Council England funded the Vayu Naidu Intercultural Storytelling Theatre from 2001-2012. Her work is digitally archived by SADAA, the South Asian Diaspora Arts and Archives. Her plays and music have been broadcast and staged.

Vayu Naidu's previous novel, *Sita's Ascent* (2013), was nominated for the Commonwealth Book Award. She lives in London with her husband, as well as at Mammallapuram. She can be found online at www.vayunaidu.com.

The Sari
of
Surya Vilas

~*a novel*~

Vayu Naidu

SPEAKING
TIGER

SPEAKING TIGER PUBLISHING PVT. LTD
4381/4 Ansari Road, Daryaganj,
New Delhi–110002, India

First published in paperback by Speaking Tiger 2017

ISBN: 978-93-86338-09-9
eISBN: 978-93-86338-00-6

10 9 8 7 6 5 4 3 2 1

Typeset in Adobe Jenson Pro by SÜRYA, New Delhi
Printed at Thomson Press India Ltd.

For

Chris Banfield and the constancy of Love across lost continents
Arundhati Menon—a constant star and dream weaver
Usha Aroor—my raft across all this time
Aban and Jaya, Dad and Mum so it all began with you
Swami Tripurananda—for the Stillness before
Thakur and Ma and the secret of Silence.

'As a woman I have no country. As a woman I want no country. As a woman, my country is the whole world.'
—*Virginia Woolf*

'…a language cannot be reduced to a dictionary or stock of words and phrases. Nor can it be reduced to a warehouse of the works written in it. A spoken language is a body; a living creature; whose physiognomy is verbal and whose visceral functions are linguistic. And this creature's home is the inarticulate as well as the articulate.'
—*John Berger*

'*Vaadala Vaadala Venta Vaadavo*…from the five elements He made thread, with our diverse temperaments the colours were dyed. Imagine! We are given the loom to weave our saris, our life…'
—Attributed to *Annamacharya*

'To articulate what is past does not mean to recognise "how it really was". It means to take control of a memory, as it flashes in a moment of danger.'
—*Walter Benjamin*, 'On the Concept of History'

Book One

Perfect Timing

Madras, December 1909

Dharma tapped the hood three times with the ivory lion of his Malacca cane. He was on a mission and timing was crucial. The rickshaw puller, sweat and salt lines pouring down his back and legs, slowed his running to a stop at the gatepost. The wooden rickshaw (made in China) and its Indian passenger were skillfully set down without a judder. Dharma paid a pice for the four-mile journey and then looked at the wide dial of his B.W. Raymond pocket watch. The second hand was racing with railway punctuality toward a minute past rahu kalam, the inauspicious hour. On Saturdays, like today, it was from 9:00 to 10:30 in the morning. Perfect timing. 10:31. He snapped the watch shut and crossed the threshold of astrology's malefic powers into an auspicious time zone. Dharma peered at the Madras winter sun; being native, to him it was chill at 72 degrees. He walked purposefully past the gateposts of *Surya Vilas*. The eucalyptus trees created an evergreen wall between the busy traffic on the High Road and the curved driveway to the house. Allarmelu, his niece, and Kanna, Cook's daughter, were playing in the round garden bordered with red hibiscus in front of the family home.

Even at that distance, he could hear the grandfather clock chiming the half-hour in the dining hall. He saw the two girls pull up their pavadai skirts to their calves. His niece Allarmelu led the dance and its rhyme:

'hickory dickory docku, mousu clocku poushindi
clocku okita strikeindi, mousu kinda parigithindhi

and Kanna shouted with glee, *'ickory dickory docku!'*

When the clock stopped chiming, the girls became statues, and after a count of ten, continued what they were doing earlier. Dharma saw Allarmelu flick the water off the strand of jasmines as she tied them to Kanna's hair. They both were nine years old and yet, Kanna seemed quicker to move and slower to speak, and would never raise her eyes to address anyone. Allarmelu slid a hairpin into Kanna's plait to firmly secure a second strand of orange and purple flowers. Then she whirled Kanna round to face her.

'Promise me you'll remember it's '*Hh*', *Hickory*, not *ickory dickory docku*. Say '*Hh*'; otherwise it sounds really pannade, vulgar, as if you are a country bumpkin. Now go, I've taught you all you need to know!' Kanna scampered off, the sound of her anklet bells jingling long after she turned the corner into Cook's house.

It was the morning of the annual winter picnic. The masala grinder, the vegetable chopper and the runner carried grains, curried meat and vegetables in brass and copper cauldrons to the coach at the far end of the driveway, near the stable. It was parked behind the shiny carriage that would drive the family and its guests to Edward Elliot's Beach for the picnic. The milkman, who was supervising the logistics, felt very important as he shouted to the food-laden men to make sure nothing should spill. The horses were whisking their tails and flicking the seasonal rain-flies off their ears. Yet more servants were scurrying about, loading the puddings and kulfis into a compartment at the rear of the coach.

Dharma watched the coachman draining a tall brass tumbler. How he too ached for a long drink of buttermilk, seasoned with cumin, salt, fresh curry leaves and grated ginger. It would settle his stomach after last night's indulgences at the Victoria Club. Fortunately, he had vomited his stomach empty; his head stuffed with dreams. He gazed at the cawing peacock strutting in the garden with its shimmering tail barely touching the ground, 'rich, beautiful, so bourgeois and bloody bulky', he muttered.

Allarmelu stretched her bare arms out toward the sky. The peacock's cry always gave her goose pimples. She heard tapping from the window of her mother's room upstairs. Mother and daughter waved to each other. Allarmelu glowed with wellness and smiled.

Dharma sneaked up and held Allarmelu's arm in mid-air. She jumped around to face her captor with both arms latticed over her head. It was a trick that uncle and niece played repeatedly. Dharma knelt, crackling his starched crisp white cotton dhoti.

'My golden Bangaru! All dressed up. But what's this? Silk pavadai and blouse, flowers in the hair, gold chain and waistband, and bare arms? How can we have our rich little Allarmelu so poorly turned out? What will your future husband say, *A bride with NO bangles?* Che che! Let's see how we can sort this out.' He poked at her waist and they both laughed. She pouted.

'But how, Chinnaina?' she said, considering her bare arms in preparation of something called 'a husband'. He held her right elbow, straightening her forearm and curling the fine hair on it. They were golden.

'You see, I am going to turn your hair into gold. Close your eyes.'

She did. He deftly took the ruby-red velvet pouch from his jubba shirt pocket and swiftly slipped one gold bangle studded with pearls onto her hand and drew it up to her forearm. When she opened her eyes she was in bangle heaven. *It doesn't matter*, he thought, *even though they were intended for…nothing goes to waste. Rule number one: a gift like this comes in handy.* His pocket watch slipped out. Allarmelu snapped it open. Dharma saw time slipping away as he fumbled to put the empty pouch back into his jubba.

'Have you had your milk?' He was concerned; if Allarmelu had not drunk her milk, the departure for the picnic would be further delayed.

'It was too sweet. I poured it into the hedge.' Another pout.

'How will you be strong and smart enough to play cricket then?'

That was enough. Allarmelu skipped her way in Kanna's direction, intent on showing off her bangle in the kitchen and drinking a whole tumbler of milk in one long gulp without stopping for air, while Dharma walked into the house.

He had to speak to Chellamma, Allarmelu's mother, urgently. It was just his style to find the most unconsidered moment, as this one, to have a conference about a seriously significant matter. It had yielded great success in the past, partly due to his timing, but more due to the impatience of others to get on with their task at hand, which he was interrupting. They would give in to his request through sheer exasperation. He did not necessarily remind anyone that he was the youngest in a family of fourteen children and that his siblings had effectively brought him up when their mother died. His helplessness was genuine, charismatic even, at twenty-three.

Dharma was the youngest of twelve surviving children. His mother died delivering a stillborn, who would have been her fourteenth. As a motherless child, he was indulged by aunts and older relatives, much to the chagrin of his siblings. Armed with the family silver spoons, every known appetite of his was met without the least effort; his role effectively became one of a playboy. Dharma enjoyed fine taste and excellent social circles, thanks to Jagan, his older brother, who had set up the first modern south Indian export of animal skins to Germany—crocodile, snake, goat and buffalo. Jagan's shrewd business sense had never clouded his notion that Chellamma, his only wife, and Allarmelu, their only child, were beyond doubt the real gems in his life; they were the pillars of happiness that *Surya Vilas* was founded on. Dharma admired his older brother's good judgment and luck. He was also intimidated by Jagan's quick temper at laziness masquerading as bad luck.

Dharma's finely sculpted nose, shock of ebony curls drizzling over his high forehead and brown expressive eyes—often mistaken for being considerate—opened doors to secrets, particularly when he was with women. His immaculate selection of attar to suit the perfume of each season often heralded him into gatherings, where other, more powerful men would be made to feel awkward. His calling card was a small ruby-red velvet pouch of loose, pink freshwater pearls, or the occasional gold bangle.

He had entered *Surya Vilas*, the stately house inherited by Jagan, a house that their father built. His sister-in-law Chellamma had made it a home for relatives near and far. The light streamed onto the sandstone yellow-washed walls and pillars through the red, green, yellow, and indigo-blue glass panels in the arch of the Georgian doorway. The last wisps of smoke hung in the air from the neem-leaf fumigation, to keep mosquitoes away. He crossed the harlequin floor and steadied himself on the teak staircase with its mock baroque balustrade. He hoped this would be the last wave of nausea from the excesses of inebriation the night before.

As he ascended the stairs, he gazed almost in salutation at portraits of his ancestors, mostly men in turbans with pearls and plumes, holding tightly wound scrolls. Dharma was adept at avoiding the creak on the stair in the middle landing and went up two steps at a time. He couldn't resist inspecting the most fetching subject, whom he resembled the most. He paused. This great-uncle of his had died when he was twenty-nine, of typhus. He was the only one with a military affiliation. The 80th Carnatic Regiment had honoured him for supplying medical remedies for snakebite to the troops quelling insurgents on the Coromandel Coast. *Such beauty, immortal!* Dharma thought. He avoided the next two steps as there was a well-known creak on one of them. His swift movement made his stomach lurch again. He bowed at the Tanjore paintings of the gods, particularly Rama and Sita at their coronation. Then, he came upon the sole portrait of a female member of the family. Only Jagan could tame tradition by taking his wife out of the customary purdah, and have her portrait painted. She was suitably wheat-complexioned, with a high, almost protuberant forehead. Her thick black hair was parted off-centre fashionably, unlike most women her age. The artist had insisted she smile, showing her teeth; very daring for a respectable married woman. Even the renowned Raja Ravi Varma's portraits of Hindu goddesses and courtesans had their gaze fixed in the near distance or at a musical instrument or symbolic bird—never directly at the viewer. But here, the artist, who was heavily influenced by the master's style, made a departure by having Chellamma look straight at the viewer from her almond-shaped eyes under her well-defined eyebrows, with a wide smile. The artist had captured her spontaneity, which had endeared her to the pantheon of Jagan's dependents, Dharma and his sisters being among them.

When he came to the landing he saw himself in the long gilt-edged mirror. He paused, his right foot not yet resting beside his left on the red coir carpeted landing. He was shocked. The light from the long window on the left clearly showed him a voluptuous red stain of paan juice on his collar. *Damn*, he bit his lip, *how do I explain this!*

Last night flooded back. The Italian gentleman Beppo who was introduced to him at the Victoria Club knew a few words of Tamil. *Impressive*, Dharma had observed; a European taking care to learn the native language. Dharma found Beppo's enthusiasm for Chola bronze, and Mahabalipuram stone sculpture striking. But his admiration inclined even more toward the Italian's impeccable sartorial taste. Perfectly tailored suit, cufflinks and cravat. Beppo seemed to know how to keep the ladies flattered, by constantly referring to himself as 'Your servant' with them, while never for one moment losing control of the women who were in his care. Russian women. Dancers trained in the Ballet in Russia, who gave such daring performances.

After dinner, the French doors opened out on to the verandah. Women returned from powdering their noses wisened by new gossip and continued in whispers behind their hand fans. Men strolled out to smoke and acquaint themselves with local business, liaisons, and indeed, all the news that concerned Empire. Beppo looked at Dharma.

'Does kartikai keep the eyes cool? And the red stain on your lips…'

Dharma took out his little silver case with the tightly rolled paan leaves filled with sweet, juicy and opiate condiments.

'An aphrodisiac?'

Beppo and Dharma's eyes met the way a river bridges civilizations. Beppo picked up the paan with his thumb and index finger, fashionably stained with tobacco, placed it between his lips like a cigar, and then bit the paan. After a good amount of chewing, and when he saw that there was no sign of the disdain that most Europeans wore on their faces against the dreaded and versatile paan, Dharma confidently mentored Beppo in its delights. After the juices had rolled over his tongue, Dharma showed him that 'there are ways of speaking, and singing with it'.

Then they were swaying, and the world seemed a

friendlier place. The opium and wine were swirling through their bloodstream. Dharma and Beppo had crossed the frontier of differences; now they were galloping across a plain of playfulness the way confident men who are comfortable with affluence, without its responsibility, can. They were laughing and as Beppo faced Dharma, he said 'Amore!' and a ripe squirt of paan juice shot past him in an arc into the verandah. Dharma was evidently within range for the paan stain to have hit his collar.

The night had run on and Beppo discreetly invited Dharma to his apartments, where they smoked and drank and talked business. Beppo was looking for a provider for the costumes and forthcoming production of an emerging company that was receiving critical acclaim and public attention. Dharma proclaimed himself as the man who could make all this happen, as he felt passionate about their dance.

Another wave of nausea and Dharma came out of his reverie. He whipped out his ivory-toothed comb encased in its silver filigree frame. Looking at himself in the gilt-edged mirror on the landing, he combed through his centre-parted ebony curls, thinking. Then he combed through his pencil-thin moustache for more time to think. The seconds were peeling away, as the scurrying down below to get everything ready for the picnic reminded him. He walked toward the window on the top landing and saw the smoke rising. The kitchen roof was hidden by the plantain grove from where he was standing; its chimney billowing forth the aroma of finely diced onions tossed in sizzling pure ghee with bay leaves and cinnamon bark.

'Now! Now, just think of now.' He polished his diamond earrings and the five onyx buttons on his jubba with his handkerchief and adjusted his dhoti till the fine strand of gold amid the green braided border shone. His brow furrowed. How was he going to ask Chellamma for the loan, with this unmistakable stain on his collar? It would have been permissible if he had been with his mistress, Lali, last night. But everyone knew she was convalescing after she had the baby, and no one discussed it. Dharma couldn't help feeling 'it'—the affair, the mistress, and the baby which had all been tied together in one lump—loomed like an empress-sized mosquito net that was never open for discussion in the family, who therefore assumed it was hidden from public gaze. His wealth detached him from 'it' while his itinerant heart was attached to 'it'. Dharma had been sliced out of Jagan's official books and had it not been for Chellamma's intervening, he would never have been reinstated to receive his monthly allowance in spite of not working. Dharma invested some of it in horoscopes for the improvement of his aspirations toward independence.

Jagan had been gracious to include him in the picnic gathering today. Chellamma could never allow any family member to be excluded, and she encouraged, possibly even indulged, Dharma's artistic pursuits by saying, 'If as family we don't support his artistic inclination, how will he survive? One day it will bear fruit.' Looking at the stain on his collar he felt another wave of nausea and swallowed hard. He couldn't afford to let them think he had taken on another mistress, especially after the baby of the first one. While his brother disapproved, Chellamma lavished gifts on the newborn and its mother secretly, because births and beginnings to life were a source of joy to her. And today Dharma hadn't brought the customary strand of jasmines and coconut offerings from the Parthasarathi temple to appease everyone. He fidgeted with his gold rings as he replaced the comb deep in his jacket's side pocket.

How could he explain being with Beppo last night? For Dharma, Beppo was new, a rough diamond, unheard of, who had brought a world that was not British, at the doorstep of Madras. He had brought Russian women. And these women revolutionized the spectator's way of viewing dance. These women danced with such ferocity and bare lily-white arms. They did not tip their toes in satin shoes. They danced bare-foot. They had such pride in their classical training. Their toenails were painted red like their lips, and their strong hair was boldly worn loose, lining their finely spun substantial bodies. They smelt of roses, bringing the fragrance of faraway so close…. He suddenly felt a sharp edge in the jacket pocket. He had it. A spare collar.

The door to the right was open and the cream-coloured crochet lace curtain fluttered. Dharma gave a spectacular cough to announce his arrival in the upstairs library, where women ruled. He nearly kicked himself as he quickly muffled it with his monogrammed kerchief to ensure there were no more untimely accidents with a spray of red juice, even if he wasn't chewing on a paan at the moment.

Picnic At Elliot's Beach

'Dharma, no need to lurk! Your shoes creak. Especially when you creep up the stairs, we know it's you.' It was his older sister Gowri. He had barely parted the crochet curtain when her gaze fixed him at the door. She was seated at the round teak table with newspapers spread on it, a magnifying glass with an ebony handle to one side.

'I hope you're coming to the picnic? Allarmelu will pout and sulk if you don't. That could ruin it for all of us.'

'Of course! Did you doubt it?' he said as he straightened his jubba sleeves.

'You seem very busy these days? Investment, at last?' came from their older sister Ruku in her inimitable nasal tone that had won her the nickname of 'nosey Nambiar' merely for the sake of alliteration.

Dharma had concluded that these sisters of his were mirrors of each other. They thought, ate, dressed alike, in spite of their dissimilar dimensions, casting the spell of prehistoricity around them. In brief, anything with life or spontaneity withered within seconds of their gaze. While Gowri was fat and was visibly a lover of sweets, Ruku was bamboo-reed thin, yet greedy and overactive. They both were dressed in pea-green satin saris with peach-coloured Belgian lace trimmings decoratively pinned with silver butterfly brooches around the napes of their white leg-of-mutton sleeved blouses. It was evident that sensible sartorial taste or beauty had not been gifted to them. Dharma decided it was their good fortune to remain unaware of it. However, they hoped their uniformity in attire would attract the attention of family and friends while they promenaded during the picnic on Elliot's Beach. They had secretly rehearsed their ascent and descent from their designated coach on the footstool under the table.

Dharma picked a pista-encrusted laddu from the silver dish on the table beside the broadsheets; he needed sweetness in a room where lightness was blighted.

'Investment? Yes... you could say it's a new investment for our family business...actually, I must speak to Chellamma anni.' He eyed *The Times* lying on the table, and noticed Gowri had placed the magnifying glass on an advertisement:

Lemos Patent Lemon clip:
John Barker & Co. Jewellery Department.
The crowning Adjunct to your table. Practical, hygienic,
Ornamental. The lemon juice goes just where required.
No more soiled fingers or tablecloths.

Webster's, the dog-eared dictionary, was beside it. It was evident that Gowri was not going to order an electroplated lemon-clip from Kensington High Street, all that way away in England. Even Dharma, who had scarcely entered a kitchen, knew it had absolutely no function in the grand tradition of Indian cuisines. She was, however, endeavouring to find what 'adjunct' meant when placed next to 'crowning'. The dictionary was the wrong place to start, he knew, as a one-time student of English Literature. Younger brother and older sister looked at each other. He smiled with his eyes identifying her deficiency, and she lowered her gaze feeling diminished.

The Tamil edition of *The Hindu* was closer to Gowri. She never liked to admit she could read only the Tamil edition fluently, as being seen to read the English paper would have afforded her higher esteem. Dharma often wondered what she was trying to prove as a woman in a world ruled by men? 'T'was ever thus, and t'will ever be, woman will ever look up to man, Q.E.D!' he had repeatedly closed quarrels between them.

'Did you hear the news at the Club? We're going to get a new government office near Mint and it's going to be named after Lord Ripon.' Gowri was persistent that she *had* read the English edition of *The Madras Standard*.

'Not only that! At last, they've named Black Town "Georgetown!" That's after the Prince of Wales' visit to the Fort. That'll be good for the family business too, and who knows, you might even find a proper office?' Of course, it was Ruku. Her principal source of information was the vegetable seller who brought fresh produce for *Surya Vilas* from Flower Bazaar in Black Town. He lived with his cart, without rent, in a building next to the stables in the *Surya Vilas* compound. The vegetables were accompanied by juicy gossip from Moore Market near the railway station.

'Not bad, although you are in purdah, you seem to get a lot of news. Very good.' Dharma shrugged at the display of information by Ruku and Gowri as if it was shallow. But he took a mental note of it, and ensured nothing he uttered would disclose he was frequenting

Victoria Club. Dharma was getting fidgety that his sisters were surpassing his ability as the family 'news reporter'. 'More buildings, more contracts. Yes, there'll be so much to do. We may never have time for living any more. Only business. So, the Picnic…is everything ready?'

'You must learn to wait,' the sisters chorused.

Ramulu, Cook's husband and consummate server entered, offering a silver tray of hot murku to the sisters. Dharma hadn't eaten. His sisters plucked at the pile. They munched their way through the diminishing murku, looking at him with lidless eyes before they snapped yet another limb off the rice pretzels. They jutted their jaws toward the tray that Ramulu held. Dharma had learned that the prehistoric gaze and jaw jutting toward an item of food was a gesture indicating 'have-some-quickly-otherwise-it-will-be-dismembered-and-demolished'.

Then with a flutter of the lace curtains, and a cloud of sandalwood fragrance, the deadening scene in the room changed to vitality.

'My goodness, Dharma!' came Chellamma's refreshing voice as she walked into the room, her girdle ring jingling with multiple keys. She was settling the pleats to her lilac Mysore georgette sari. Allarmelu ran toward him holding up her right arm with the oversized bangle he had just given her. Her aunts looked suspiciously at the ornament and then at Dharma. Chellama seemed either oblivious to this or intent on feeding her family again after breakfast. 'Come, you dear soul! It's too early and you wouldn't have had any breakfast! Ramulu, some upumau for Dharma aiya and kapi for all of us, please?' It was time for tiffin. The ritual of drinking the age-old, home-ground Plantation A and Peabury blend coffee mixed with chicory and hot milk *had* to be followed before embarking on the annual winter picnic.

Dharma gave a warm sigh as he saw Chellamma. 'My brother is the luckiest man alive to wake up to her,' he thought. His sisters stood protectively around Chellamma their sister-in-law, lest his gaze tarnish her brightness. They watched over her and continued crunching on their murku.

Relieved that the atmosphere had lifted, he found himself saying, 'I'm so glad we are all going together. Allarmelu, look! I've even ordered for the tennicoit and net to be loaded in the coach so we can play. Oh! What would we ever do without Elliot's Beach? The lungs of our beloved Madras...'

'We must make the most of the weather now. Your brother tells us a lot of changes are afoot in government. At least today will give us all time to have a reunion with family and friends, maybe even rest...' Chellamma never uttered Jagan's name, as a mark of respect even while speaking to his relatives.

'Chellamma, *you* need to relax, Dharma is always in the resting position!' Gowri ended with a sneer. This elicited a grunt of laughter from Ruku. Something in Chellamma's presence brought out a juvenility in Jagan's siblings. It was possible that she took notice of the underlying competitiveness for her affection among these three. Ruku and Gowri, for their part, would die for their sister-in-law. When Ruku had become a widowed bride at the age of fourteen, a tonsured head and work as a menial hidden from public gaze in her paternal uncle's home was the future that awaited her. Gowri, who was younger than her and inseparable, was rejected from marriage proposals as it was assumed she carried her sister's bad luck on her head. The matchmakers put the word out in the matrimonial market.

Chellamma, heavily pregnant with Allarmelu, set out in a carriage at rahu kalam in the heat of the afternoon to Jagan's Uncle's home where the sisters were locked in a forgotten musty room at the rear of the house. She knew it was a time when everyone except the cook would be asleep. Unlocking their room, she packed their trunks and without consulting Jagan, brought his sisters to stay at *Surya Vilas*. No one dared to censure Chellamma's action, as they were terrified of Jagan's wrath. Ruku and Gowri's future, which could have concluded in solitary confinement, insanity or indeed suicide, was branded in their memory. Their loyalty to Chellamma was total, as was her love for them. But Gowri and Ruku were jealous of the affection that she showed Dharma, and he grudged their proximity to her. So there was never a portrait of familial bliss when they were all together. Dharma suddenly looked weary and belittled at Gowri's remark and the chorus of his sisters' laughter in front of Allarmelu. It was his turn to feel diminished.

'Dharma, we're only teasing. After all, if your sisters don't tease you, how will you face this beguiling world?' Chellamma said with charming seriousness, and resolving his feeling of abandonment. He knew Chellamma was the only one who gave his aspirations credence, even if there were never any tangible results. Jagan good-humouredly teased Dharma about being eternally youthful and therefore without responsibility, and the sisters chorused with approval. It was Chellamma who would include him in the business meetings so he could feel a sense of responsibility. Dharma valued that, but life's distractions were a necessity as far as he was concerned.

The semolina upumau arrived. Dharma dipped his hands in the fingerbowl, and dabbed them dry on the cotton towel that Ramulu handed to him, saving him the exertion of walking to the washstand a few yards away. He dived elegantly into the fare. 'Wah! Chellamma anni! The upumau your Cook makes is food for the gods! The chutney stirs the buds...'

'O Dharma, I'm so happy you're enjoying it! No greater joy than seeing my family eat with relish!' Chellamma smiled at all the members of her husband's family with contentment.

'Bangaru Chellamma!' they all heard the baritone of her husband's call from the landing downstairs. 'Come, my work is done. Let's go. Allarmelu! Where are you hiding, my girl?'

Allarmelu ran out of the room and stuck her head through the banister.

'Naina! Look!'

Jagan looked up and father and daughter winked and stuck their tongues out on cue and burst into laughter. All life resumed. Gowri and Ruku picked up their crotchet wraps, while Chellamma rushed to the landing so that her husband could see she was ready. In spite of her planning and getting the entire staff, menu and family together, it was always seen that she was the last to be ready. As Jagan stood on the harlequin floor the gardener's boy gave a final wipe to his shoes. He placed his talappa on his head and took his ebony cane with the carved silver lion handle. Everyone cascaded down the staircase toward him as he proceeded to the verandah.

The carriage was ascended and Jagan, Chellamma, Allarmelu with Dharma sat in the big shiny eight-seater. Dr Benjamin and Ashwaq Khan with his Begum Zaida formed the rest of the party. Allarmelu had a choice of laps and sat half-and-half on the women. Their perfumes of khus and roja enticed her. Counting their gold bangles and gem-studded rings became an enticing arithmetic lesson.

Another coach carried Gowri, Ruku, Kanna and all the food. The runner, and Ramulu stood on the ramp to serve at the picnic.

Dharma's heart sank as the journey started. The swaying of the carriage lulled and made him anxious in turns. The conversation between the women and the men was at times collective, and otherwise in pairs. Men spoke in English. Allarmelu had completely ignored Dharma as he watched her consumed in adoration of the women. He noticed how these women spoke in fairly hushed tones mixing Telugu with Deccani, punctuated with English adjectives. So different from the women he met in Beppo's charge last night. The Russians laughed with their heads thrown back, and didn't cover their mouths the way Indian women did. They had looked straight into Dharma's eyes when they asked questions about India. They flew between extremes of expressing how they loved and hated aspects of their visit to India. That vigour, that rigour, he found in their dance. A total self-belief in perfection. He wanted to belong to *that*.

As he looked on and listened, Dharma was scheming a plan to speak to Chellamma alone. He needed a loan. Plain money, and silk, plenty of it, from her family's weavers at Seeraivakkam. She was the only one who

would understand what he saw in real art. She was the
one who saw potential in his incomplete poems and his
need for independence. The clicking of the horses' hooves
seemed to make his thoughts whirr and the excitement
heighten. Beppo was his horizon. Inspired by him,
Dharma could feel the urgency for a new life. But his
greater fear at the moment was not the sacrifice of great
art, but his acceptance in Beppo's circle. He had to hurry
to make a claim. Otherwise Beppo would cast him out
of the revolutionary cultural event of the century—an
emerging Ballet from Russia. It was the talk of the town
at the European clubs.

Why not ask his brother Jagan directly, Dharma
thought? He tried to picture the scene. He could hear
Jagan's words ringing in his head.

'*Yentra nu? You're a fine fellow! You attempted BA
English Honours and failed, at least you passed in airs and
graces, now you want to set up a song-and-dance company
is it?*'

He knew Jagan would see right through him. It wasn't
really about setting up a business or an investment for
the family's future. The home truth was that Dharma
needed the money because he lied to Beppo that he could
finance the costumes of the forthcoming production of
this newly formed, imperially supported company. Beppo
was scouting for original materials, particularly southern
Indian silk. Attracted by Madame Blavatsky's legacy of
interracial spiritualism in Madras, Beppo was on a visit
to seek pure hand-woven silk and an authentic eastern
motif; a perfect design for costume and backdrop for
the forthcoming ballet that would tour Europe. Where
better than India?

When Beppo and Dharma met, it was a natural attraction; neither was interested in money, only in the magnetizing whirl of social meetings and the exchange of ideas, which they could revolve around in—and consequently, what delirious change it could bring. Beppo had opened Dharma's eyes to a dance and music that was at the edge of change, and its women and men. He didn't understand it, it was so heady. He felt he had a part in the wider world, as an equal player. He ached for change and a fantastical need for independence.

At the crossing to Elliot's Beach, which was a part of the Marina closer to the serene end of San Thome Cathedral, the convoy slowed down. Dharma came out of his reverie. The voices of the men droned on, and he remained silent out of deference.

The beach sand was like golden crumbled biscuit. The sea breeze relieved the humidity and took the sting out of the noonday heat. Dharma was enticed by the foam of the sea, stretching far, and folding in wide skirts, as each diagonal wave thudded on the shore. Another two coaches of Jagan's associates and Chellamma's family friends met the picnic party. The coachmen and Ramulu had marked a spot that was partly shaded by coconut palms. The temple-elephant printed pandal marquee was hoisted with the help of eager local labour. Carpets were laid out first and then the chairs and teepoys. The wood fires were set up some distance away to heat the cauldrons of fresh crab korma, paya with goat's trotters and testicles, Uzbek loaves, and Hyderabad biriyani with tamarind curried prawns, masala liver, fried kidneys, and shahi tukda for dessert.

Dharma who managed to busy himself without

assisting anyone was visible and within earshot. He
decided to start the game of tennicoit. He made Gowri
and Ruku one team. They sat on chairs, while he threw
the ring on their behalf and they caught it, like two
chained terriers, if it fell within their arc of the 'court'
on the beach. In the opposing team, across the net, were
Kanna and Allarmelu running breathless to catch his
balletic throws.

Dr Benjamin, a Syrian Christian of Malayali descent,
educationist and Professor of English, settled himself in
his cane deck chair and began smoking his pipe. Jagan
was in a good mood as his Chellamma was around.

'So Docgaru, how has this past year fared in your
opinion, following the Morley-Minto reforms?' Jagan was
skillful in opening conversations that would not border
on superficialities.

'Well, it's only just been announced. It is yet to be
legislated. Doubtless, something has to be said for
Ripon's foresight before he left. He made Madras a local
government. The diarchy won't do us harm,' Dr Benjamin
replied.

'That too a few years after the King's visit. Black Town
being renamed Georgetown makes me wonder if this is
recognition of us as responsible Indians, or dismissal. I
can only hope it is good for business,' said Jagan looking
at his open palm as if he was reading his fortune.

Ashwaq was shelling pistas he had brought from
his recent visit to Kandahar. 'Jagan anna, after that
Foundation ceremony, at the Clubs there's talk that the
Corporation of Madras building is going to be named
after Lord Ripon.'

'Well it's because of him they are mooting local

government in Madras Presidency. But we must also see the emergence of the Justice Party.' Jagan looked enquiringly at Dr Benjamin.

Dr Benjamin sighed. 'It'll probably be the only hope for all of us who are non-Brahmins.'

'Gandhi's call in South Africa is gaining power over people. And he's making sure that Hindus and Muslims are seeing themselves as Indians.' Jagan slurped the tender coconut water given to him and picked at the pistas.

'That Black Immigration act is nothing but a system to enrage everyone, and make sure each one of the natives is identified, and that we move in slow traffic. It's like cattle counting.' Dr Benjamin leaned over to accept Ashwaq's offering of raisins and pistas. The men laughed.

'To tell you the truth, Ripon building will be good for us. The engineers want all the interiors in teak. Joists, pillars, landings, almost all surfaces, and then there's the furniture too, Inshallah!' Ashwaq added with a note of optimism.

'Wah Ashwaqbai! That will keep you going for generations together! Inshallah!' Jagan raised a toast with the sweet coconut water.

Dr Benjamin was listening attentively and proceeded to swat a fly with his neatly folded newspaper. He swiftly unfolded it. 'Did you read Gandhi's preface to Tolstoy's letter in *New Hindustan*? Here, let me read it to you. I couldn't resist bringing it:

'"*Do not resist evil, but also do not yourselves participate in evil—in the violent deeds of the administration of the law courts, the collection of taxes and, what is more important, of the soldiers, and no one in the world will enslave you.*"

'Who can question the truth of what he says in the

following: *"A commercial company"*—he means the East
India Company—*"enslaved a nation comprising two
hundred millions. Tell this to a man free from superstition
and he will fail to grasp what these words mean. What
does it mean that thirty thousand people, not athletes, but
rather weak and ordinary people, have enslaved two hundred
millions of vigorous, clever, capable, freedom-loving people?
Do not the figures make it clear that not the English, but the
Indians, have enslaved themselves?"'*

'Tolstoy!' Dharma found himself blurting out. Ashwaq
and Jagan were digesting the reading, each in turn
wondering whose side Tolstoy really was on. Indians
were daily being humiliated with one encroachment or
the other by British rule and Tolstoy's grand reasoning
negated Indian humility.

Dr Benjamin looked up from the newspaper and
glared benignly at his BA-Honours-attempted-but-failed
ex-student. 'A memory of literature welling up, Dharma?'
he enquired, and Jagan and Ashwaq winked at each other.

'Nn-o...Professor. It was just that I was making a
Russian connection. The Tsar has, I'm given to believe,
given his approval of a Ballet led by a certain gentleman
called Diaghilev. Absolute magic. I mean, of course I
haven't seen it... I saw the posters. Real art...' was all
that could tumble out. Dharma was in love with Russia
because Beppo came with it and the chance of change
came with its wave of difference. He had twisted threads
together in his head about Tolstoy and ballet.

'I think Madam Blavatsky has a lot to answer for when
it comes to change,' said Jagan and waved to Chellamma.
She and Begum Zaida were rising and dipping in the
beach sand as they approached them. 'I don't know why

every foreigner who comes to India loves to set up so many institutions and counter-institutions. A lot of money going into the railways, but no benefit for the passenger. I hope it doesn't drain all our money and means in the name of an institution. Blavatsky and her team have set up an institution in the spirit realm called the Theosophical Society. One way of breaking cultural superiority down. But of course, it's like any club—you need membership. What next!'

'Can we ever imagine an India without British masters? At least in our lifetime?' asked Dr Benjamin.

'I hope so, but it will need to be by constitutional reform. That's what Mrs Besant is fighting for', Jagan was emphatic. 'I don't think it's Gandhi's way. He says he does not want to use force, but he is very forceful in condemning this idea of empire.'

Chellamma had sat on the moda with her hand cupping her face as her elbow rested on her knee. She said decisively, 'Gandhiji will win. He wants women in the movement as well. That will get India to her feet; men and women and all together. See how in England, the women are also fighting for the vote?'

Begum Zaida, who had been listening intently, asked, 'what will happen to the law and order if they leave suddenly? Just our churches, mosques and temples will not keep us within limits.' There was general agreement that there would be chaos if the British left.

'There may be great forces that will divide us. But meanwhile we must hold together Jagan anna,' said Ashwaq. Jagan and Dr Benjamin knew what that meant. There were rumours that Muslims and Hindus and Christians would sever ties and even live in separate lands.

The hours billowed into late afternoon. Everyone was in a terrific mood, including Dharma. The biriyani was excellent. There was just one instance where Allarmelu and Kanna cried as Dharma teased them that it wasn't goat meat they were relishing in the biriyani, but the peacock from the garden. He had to work hard at the insistence of Chellamma to admit to the girls that he lied. The prickly moment was finally soothed by more candy floss, more singing and dancing, till the girls dried their tears and felt the salt in their mouth from the sea air. They concluded that the beach was a body and the sea its tears.

When they returned to *Surya Vilas*, the customary tea had to be drunk in the library upstairs, with Gowri, Ruku and Dharma. Chellamma heard to them recounting with hilarity all that had happened. When it was her turn, she looked up with a full smile from a sari border she was examining.

'Why can't these people darn the saris the way they used to?'

'I think you need to wear smoother anklets.'

'I know, Gowri, but that day with the puja I had to wear the ruby-studded ones. The stones in the left anklet were coming out of the setting. That's what started ripping the threads as I walked.' Chellamma made her case.

'Is that your wedding sari?' Dharma gazed longingly at the subtle gold on the border and across the pomegranate pink body of the sari. It was hand-woven, naturally, but had the perfect design.

'I know a very good weaver who will make it good as new,' he smiled to himself.

'How soon can it be done?' Chellama's urgency could be felt in the room.

'Chellama anni, for you time should be no concern…'

'It is the wedding sari, it has to be blessed again at the harvest Pongal next month,' came Ruku's retort.

'Consider it done,' Dharma said as he looked cheerily at his sister-in-law and sisters. He licked his fingers free of the almond halwa that he'd washed down with the cardamom tea. He washed his hands ceremoniously, twirling each gold ring on his little, ring and middle fingers. Then he took out his monogrammed handkerchief with a dancer's flourish and wiped the diamond, emerald and rubies on each of the rings, touching the corners of his lips. He then flicked open his engraved silver box and took a pinch of snuff.

'You're such a dandy!' Gowri said. 'I wonder when you will grow up.'

'When you see the sari perfectly done at Pongal, I will make you mark your words.'

Chellamma had carefully pleated and folded her wedding sari that her mother and grandmother had worn before her. Each succeeding generation had increased the length of the border, as women grew taller. 'You won't forget will you?' she pleaded as she gave it to Dharma.

Allarmelu burst into the library washed and talcum-powdered. 'Amma, Amma! Look I've written a poem,' she said waving her slate and chalk and ran to hug her mother. Her aunts instantly began singing the refrain from the slate. Dharma felt he had made some advance in coming across favourably, and now he would have to live with the interruptions. He was pleased. He saw Allarmelu, nuzzling her head on her mother's stomach, catching her hair on the gold key ring. Gowri and Ruku moved closer and undid her strand of hair.

Allarmelu saw the ancestral pomegranate pink silk sari with the sunset orange border interwoven with gold slide from her mother's arms into Dharma's hands. Its weight was sumptuous. She could smell its fragrance of turmeric, frankincense and sandalwood. A few dried tulasi leaves fell from the inner folds of the pallu. She felt the cool smoothness of the satin blouse around her mother's waist, and the smell of sandalwood on the moist skin of her belly. Her mother's butter-soft hands touched the back of her neck as the sari slid away. She felt the fingertips of her father's sisters adjusting her plaits on either side of her head. Allarmelu saw the soft brown eyes of her father's youngest brother resting on the sari, as the clock chimed seven that evening.

Firebird

Madras, January 1910

Over a week passed. Christmas in Madras blew over with the finest weather. Europeans were delighted that their talcum didn't form rings around their necks, and the Vaseline in their hair didn't go limp with humidity. The woodpecker had started knocking on the stump of the almond tree.

Dharma got the barber to shave him, following the most relaxing hot coconut oil massage and multani mud bath. Having dressed in jubba and dhoti, he carefully wrapped Chellama's wedding sari in white tissue paper, then folded it into a jute bag. It was overprinted in green, *Buckingham and Coromandel Mills*, with the elephant-headed Ganesha, the remover of all obstacles, centred in the arc.

The rickshaw picked him up. The route to Buckingham and Coromandel Mills enclave was fairly quiet at 11:30 in the morning. His rickshaw weaved its way past the bridge over Oteri canal, and thankfully the water was still high enough to keep the stench from the effluents of the tannery from being nauseating. He wondered why Madras didn't open a perfumery. *It would make good local business to get over these dastardly smells from dead skins.*

Dharma pinched his nose before smothering it with his perfumed handkerchief. He, of course, acquired his seasonal attar from Hyderabad and Lucknow.

The next left and, as the rickshaw turned, he saw Kuppu, the foreman amongst the weavers. He was Dharma's informant and knew everything about weaving, and that took place in the mills. Kuppu, red-eyed as he was, undid his red chequered head cloth and flagged the rickshaw to stop. 'Beppo aiya, waiting. One hour gone. Meeting him.'

Dharma hadn't expected this. Yet, it was just the kind of message he would lie awake for. Decision time, again. A precious family relic, a sari, had to be darned to earn Chellamma's trust and time was running short. Yet, the exhilaration of meeting Beppo meant that all else had to wait. Dharma knew he would need to spend time with Kuppu, who would then seek out a weaver to whom he would explain how neatly the sari must be darned. But how could he trust Kuppu and leave the sari with him till he returned? After all, it was a family heirloom with pure gold. Besides, Kuppu would go and have a drink of homemade liquor and leave the sari in some corner that would contaminate its sanctity for generations. Dharma decided the safest option would be to take it with him. He instructed the rickshaw puller to whirl round toward Perambur where the Railway Hotel was. Beppo had extended his stay there while social commitments continued at the Victoria Club, as it was a fashionably convenient address.

When he entered the Railway Hotel, Dharma was looked at not entirely without suspicion. He was never sure whether the staff recognized him out of respect, or envy. It was high noon. Sparrows were tittering in the verandah, and the crows were cawing in the fiery red spray of the gulmohur tree for the lunchtime treats that guests might scatter while eating in the open courtyard. At the Reception he announced he had an appointment and was escorted up to Room 7. Dharma knocked. The door was slightly ajar. He waited, wondering whether to cough and announce his arrival. He decided to step in.

To his surprise, there was the smell of roses. The grass mat blinds had been drawn nearly three-quarters of the way down to keep the scorching glare out, and the soft white muslin curtains rippled with the air coming in from the balcony.

Dharma clutched the bag with Ganesha for courage and comfort. He was standing in the lounge of the suite of rooms. He could see through to the boudoir. It was Valentina, one of the dancers who had performed the night before the picnic. She adjusted the girdle of peacock feathers and plumes from various Indian cockerels and studied her position in the wide mirror. Her hips moved slightly as she balanced her weight on her straightening right leg. A delay, and the plumes fluttered, creating a ripple that extended the first impulse of her movement. She arched her back till her head was perpendicular to the floor and nested among the feathers. Slowly she raised her head and lifted her right arm as her left leg stretched ninety degrees straight above her head. Dharma was breathless.

She caught sight of him in the mirror and began to disassemble out of the arabesque. 'Dharma! Bravo! You got my message! I was hoping you would come.'

'It wasn't Beppo?' Dharma walked in a stately manner to the boudoir which had mirrors on three sides.

'No, no, don't you understand? I had to use his name; otherwise there would be no chance of getting any message out. All because I am a ballerina.'

It wasn't so much that she was a ballerina; it was more to do with being a woman. Dharma knew there were enough systems in place to ghettoize Indians from the Europeans, and men in particular from women. It was all in the name of protection. And yet he knew of enough interracial affairs that lurked in the shadows of clubs, hotels, even churches. If only society would accept it as natural.

'That was very daring of you,' Dharma smiled winningly.

'You think so? Will you stay? But first, tell me, how do you like this idea of "costume"?'

'Very flattering.'

'You see, I have worked out two different positions. I'll show you. Tell me what you think.' She had rearranged the boudoir to make way for two quick steps to lurch into an arabesque, this time with her left leg arched like a wreath around her waist. She held her position for thirty seconds.

'And now, the other one, watch closely. Don't even blink!' Valentina walked with the awkwardness of a swan out of water and then before his eyes, Dharma saw an ordinary human form turn into a bird as she levered herself on her straight right leg on pointe, bent forward with her arms kneading the air, while the left leg was at 180 degrees. The plumes wafted across her thighs like streaks of flames.

'Wah! Valentina! You are transformed!'

'Then turn me back. Make me human.'

Her voice was not playful anymore. Her kartikai-rimmed grey eyes, her curly black hair that blew like smoke, struck a chord in his soul. He dropped the Ganesha bag with Chellamma's sari on the chaise longue and steadied himself as he walked to her. He held her waist from behind and she straightened like a bird emerging from the water, her arms holding a column of air as she stretched her spine; bird's wings flicking water dry. His chin was in the crook of her neck and their arms were entwined around her waist, her hands on his. They both looked in the mirror: two narcissuses coloured in Indian teak and Russian rose, echoing the ache and possibility of love.

'Oh! Dharma, I'm so tired of these suffocating parties. I want to see something of here. All I ever see is so tainted with English. You are the only real Indian I have met. Will you not take me to the heart of what is Indian? Even an Indian music concert?'

'There are other ways of getting away, and to the heart of it,' Dharma murmured as he felt her resting on both her feet, flat on the ground. She swivelled to face him. Her grey eyes and ivory skin, the peppermint on her breath, her beseeching face were doors opening. He took her face and traced the turquoise vein along her upstretched neck and chin with his right hand, then kissed her hard. With the heat of his body, his attar exuded more fragrance. He slipped the strap from her shoulder and eagerly went for her breast. He was now untangling the knot of his dhoti to come free. He nudged her toward the chaise longue.

'Wait' she said holding his hand on her breast, and undid the clasp at the waist. The girdle of plumes, red, amber, peacock blue, wafted to the floor and beneath them the subdued clink of the bejewelled clasp. She was still smiling with her bluish grey, partly broken teeth. He marvelled at how she took her right leg straight over his right shoulder. He thrust himself into her as she leapt and wrapped both her legs tightly around his waist. He felt such power as he stood on the ground and she mounted him. Her thighs gripped him. They moaned and bit and laughed with the motion and they both peaked in a momentous groan. Shrieking parrots and thudding guavas on the balcony of No. 7 broke the silence of their daze.

All Dharma kept hearing long after Valentina had uttered it, was 'will you not take me to the heart...' Stealing Valentina out without Beppo's permission would be stark insanity. Even Dharma who loved adventure would not be able to see an escape route from the scandal. He wouldn't mind if it were solely to do with him, but he had his elder brother, the family business and so much at stake. He too felt suffocated.

Over every single life hovered a ring of command holding the price of freedom to ransom. More than anything in the world Dharma wanted to succeed in this dream that Beppo held out in front of him. Freedom to travel through Europe, not as a subject, but as an equal. Here was a dance company that was thrilling in what it was going to offer to a crumbling world of opposites; religion versus science, imperialism versus independence, war versus non-violence. All he had to do to find his path to equality was open the door to the silk motifs that were held sacred. That was all Beppo asked for, and of course for the money that would finance it.

'You have that faraway look in your eyes, Dharma, if it's not possible ...'

He smoothed her wet hair which was growing increasingly turbulent with the humidity. She unclasped his hands from her buttocks as she unwound her legs from his waist. He looked at his throbbing penis as she walked across to the dressing table to get cigarettes for both of them. He knelt and picked up his dhoti. She placed the lit cigarette in his mouth. They both looked at each other as they sucked hard on their Russian cigarettes and squinted at the amber glow of the tips turning red.

'What will Beppo say?'

'Don't be too sensible. He doesn't know about us, yet. We'll have time to think of something. Won't we? First, ask yourself this: "Don't you feel alive?"'

'Like fire', Dharma sucked at the cigarette and then leaned to kiss her in streaming plumes of smoke. She inhaled, pressing herself even closer to him till their sweat stuck.

'When I first saw you dance, I tried to understand the story of the Firebird. Will you tell it to me in your way?'

'I only know of it from my childhood.' After a long pause she began and Dharma could hear the whirr of translation in her head as he heard in English what came from the language of her heart. 'How can I explain "winter" to you?' They both laughed as she said it. Then, like silk, the words flowed:

> '...And in my dreams I see myself on a wolf's back
> Riding along a forest path
> To do battle with a sorcerer-tsar Kaschei
> In that land where a princess sits under lock and key,
> Pining behind massive walls.

There gardens surround a palace all of glass;
There Firebirds sing by night
And peck at golden fruit…'

They heard the thud of fruit on the balcony. Both froze. These weren't fruit dropped by flying parrots. Dharma crept toward the balcony. Another guava was flying its way up. Dharma edged forward onto the stone railing of the balcony and saw the top of Kuppu's red head cloth. He was aiming one more guava when he caught sight of Dharma looking down at him. He threw his head back, eyes rolling with terror as he shouted, 'Saar! Beppo aiya coming! Lunch eating. Face very red. Come down now!'

All Dharma could do was look in the direction of Valentina. He couldn't make out entirely whether she covered her mouth with her hand in shock, or to blow him a kiss as he scrambled down the fire escape, with his dhoti fluttering like the white sails of a sinking ship as he fled the scene of the possibility of love.

The Sweetness of Importance

Madras, January 1910

Allarmelu awoke as suddenly as she had fallen asleep. She slapped a fly that had settled on the corner of her open mouth. After coughing and spluttering dramatically to announce she had completed her afternoon siesta, she waited for Cook and Kanna to arrive in her bedroom with a silver tumbler of hot Horlicks. While it was being cooled by being poured between the tumblers, one a yard lower than another, all three heads suddenly turned towards the sound of carriage wheels. They stopped short of the verandah, well within the view from Allarmelu's window.

Dharma stepped down from the carriage, followed by a European gentleman who removed his hat. His reddish-brown hair sat on either side of a centre parting glistening with pomade. Moustache with wax tips. White gloved hands, and a khaki-coloured, elegantly cut jacket with sharp creases along broad trousers. He took out his handkerchief and started waving away the flies and mosquitoes that gathered on the steps to the verandah, around the recently-watered crotons in terracotta pots. The wet soil made the air moist, attracting more insects.

Allarmelu was in awe. Dharma had brought home

a European friend. It meant the porcelain tea cups and silver would have to come out. She scrambled off her bed, after draining her Horlicks in one draught. She and Kanna giggled as Allarmelu plumped her face to show off how the Horlicks had left a malt mustache on her face. She let it dry and go crusty, then licked it off, making her tongue loll to the sides in bovine fashion. But time was tight and both girls followed Cook, who was muttering away about how she would be called in just a minute and how she would have to get the tea things ready and how Dharma had not warned anyone.

Once the men had been received in her father's study, Allarmelu sneaked onto the verandah and discovered from the coach driver that the visitor was one Mr Beppo Villetti who lived in the Railway Hotel, and was not just an ordinary European—he was from the land of the Pope, the great temple of the Christians.

The silver tea service was rolled in smoothly on a teak trolley with wooden wheels by Cook's husband Ramulu, now playing butler. He was dressed in fanned turban, jacket with cummerbund, starched trousers and bare feet.

Allarmelu had washed and secretly dabbed some talcum powder on her face, so her skin wouldn't shine, and she would look 'fair'. She wore an indigo silk pavadai with a mustard border interwoven with a gold braid of southern Indian temple spires. Her blouse, which ended on her hips with tiny slits on the sides, had the reverse combination—blue silk bordered sleeves and mustard with subtle gold checks on the body. She proudly wore the bangle Dharma had given her before the picnic. The bells on her silver anklets announced her arrival as she walked barefoot into her father's study. Every evening since her mother had taken to bed rest, she would keep her father company.

She saw Beppo sitting on an armchair, his legs crossed and his shoes shining like mirrors. She could see his interlocked white hands clasped around his right knee, with a signet ring on the little finger of his right hand. The only other jewelry he had was a dull gold pocket-watch chain that peeped from under his coat. He sat in the cane chair looking like a study in brown. Dharma sat on his right, and Allarmelu's father Jagan was at his desk opposite them. Both her father and uncle wore a Western shirt with the Indian dhoti and had diamond earrings, rings, gold chains, and the red-and-white Vishnu caste mark on their foreheads. Jagan had wound his spectacles around his ears and craned his neck as if to see his visitors more clearly. The piano stool to his left was reserved for Allarmelu. She always sat by his left—'where the heart is', as Jagan had told her.

It seemed that the assembly of men were silently translating in their various languages what should be the best topic of conversation. Weather? Railways? Politics—Britain, or Russia, or Italy, or India? The muslin curtains fluttered softly in the teatime sea breeze. The clear stream of orange pekoe flowing into the Austrian bone china cup pleasantly interrupted the polite silence. Allarmelu loved the blue flower pattern on the cups; flowers she had never seen in Madras gardens.

'Hello Signorina Allarmelu, your Uncle has told me so much about you!'

'Good things I hope, Signor Villeti?' Jagan asked good-humouredly.

'How could it be otherwise', Dharma plucked up the courage to add to the polite banter. Allarmelu wiggled more comfortably onto the stool.

'She's good in her sums, and making up poems. Just can't get her to learn English,' her father teased, partly to get her to say something in English.

'What a beautiful dress...I'm sorry I don't know how you say the Indian name...'

'The skirt is called pavadai and the blouse?' Dharma looked at Allarmelu

'Sokai', she said on cue.

Dharma laughed elegantly at the swift response, as Jagan stirred sugar rather vigorously into his tea, almost urging his daughter to prove she could speak in English, as befitted her upbringing in a respectable, aristocratic family.

'My father got it from Tanjavur', Allarmelu managed effortlessly.

'Tanjore, Allalu not Tanjavur. In Telugu, "ooru" means place, "−ore" for Europeans. Tanjore is very famous for its style of painting divine incarnations,' Jagan informed them. 'There, you see that image of Krishna as a baby? It has been in our family since my great-grandfather'. Jagan rose ever so slightly from his chair as he pointed in the direction of the painting with both his hands. It was in an alcove painted with temple red and white stripes, with an oil lamp lit in front of it. For years, the cornice of the alcove had been stained with carbon from the steady flame, along with the oil that had seeped onto the ledge.

'Of course! Tanj-ore! I just heard a story about an Italian connection. A priest, Catholic, came by ship, and walked from Goa to this place you mention.'

'When was this?' Dharma grew genuine again.

'I think it must have been after the Renaissance. He was fascinated by the noise and the worship, and procession in the streets. He was very hot, and fainted. A man passing by gave him water, and then some rice. When the priest revived, he gave the man some blue charcoal chalk, as he had no money. The man was an artist and started drawing. And the indigo colour started bleeding on the paper with the perspiration from the artist's hands. He added water, and the colour washed across the paper. The priest must have said: "Ah! Belissimo! The blue background—like the Scroveni chapel!"'

'What a wonderful story about the background colour to the Krishna paintings!' Jagan was taken by the story. He mused that the blue of Krishna signified infinity; for Krishna's devotees, it meant he was timeless and would be there throughout the ages. Jagan connected, like a devotee would, with the story showing how Krishna's presence across time was being endorsed: in a tale told by an Italian, about a Christian monk, who inspired a Hindu Tanjavur craftsman to be inventive in his technique— creating a tradition of the blue that symbolized the infinity of Krishna.

'Truly wonderful! I have even heard some people refer to it as "Venetian" blue.' Dharma was convinced.

Allarmelu listened with her eyes wide, barely breathing. She could not believe that there was a time before the time that her father and mother lived. The oldest relative she had seen was a grandmother, but that too in a photograph, in black and white. The portraits along the stairway didn't seem like real men to her. Here, grown men were sitting swapping stories about another time and the evidence they had was the blue background in the Tanjavur Krishna painting. She stopped herself from giggling. If her father or uncle passed by her mother and aunts telling stories about real people, the men would chorus: 'Don't you women have any work to do? Gup-shupping on stories, and that too about other people!'

Her real fascination was that there could be so many names to a colour she knew as 'blue'. She had always known blue as 'Krishna'; her mother had taught her his music drew the hearts of everyone to him. She didn't know what god was, but because so many animals and people were in his care, maybe that's what made him a god. Blue was a person, and then a colour. Now Krishna had so many blues to him.

She watched her uncle step comfortably across into the European's language, and manners. Her father was comfortable in speaking the European's language, but she felt comfortable in the fact that he spoke of things she knew—Tanjavur, Krishna, and now the delicious murku that had arrived with the badam halwa. She felt very proud, as these were her favourites and all the gentlemen agreed the combination of flavours was 'excellente!'

Then came the dreadful moment when her father said: 'Allalu, go fetch your fiteel and sing a quick song for our guest.'

'Oh! Signorina! You are so expressive without saying a word! How your face showed such horror like an Arlechino, after such a delightful instruction!'

'She can play the violin, but practice is what she doesn't perfect,' Dharma frowned at Allarmelu in mock reprimand.

'I have a poem. But you must join in.'

'Wah!' the men chorused.

Kanna peeped through the doorway, only her head showing, full of red and yellow ribbons. Allarmelu and she exchanged glances. Kanna looked close to tears. Allarmelu was going to sing the poem that both of them made up. It was *their* poem, and Allarmelu was parading it to the elders.

'Kanna, why are you peeping? Come and say it with Allalu.'

Kanna scampered in and bowed to Jagan, delighted at his instruction and stood behind Allarmelu. Allarmelu sat up straight on the piano stool. 'Ready? You must join in at the clicks with what I say.'

Allarmelu: *Bun, bun*

Kanna: *Yenna bun?*

Click

Male chorus: *Bun bun*

Kanna: *Jam bun*

Allarmelu: *Yenna tea*

Click

Male chorus: *Yenna tea*

Kanna: *Ponda tee!*

Allarmelu: *and Tea party!*

Click.

Male chorus: *and Tea party!*

The words may have been lost in translation, but none of the fun. Kanna's pun about 'pondatee' (wife) was acknowledged by Allarmelu as clever but not useful in a situation she had quickly realized had to undergo translation. She was pleased—she'd conducted an event and won the approval of her father, in the company of gentlemen who ruled the world. That gave her a whole wave of confidence that made her want to defy the need for learning to speak English. Why couldn't people speak in Telugu, Urdu or Tamil as well?

Beppo's cries of 'Bravo! Encore!' became even more thrilling when he brought out a lacquered box painted in red, black and gold. On the lid was an exotic bird with a gold fruit in its beak and another held in its talon. All the sides of the box overflowed with its red and gold plumes. It glistened. Beppo held it on display in his large, smooth hands. 'For you Signorina, for your hospitality, and recital.'

The rebellion didn't last long. Allarmelu was in wonderland. She had decided she would learn English and European and speak fluently in all of them. She would sing in them and invite all these people to her house and everybody would say she was the greatest host on earth. She instinctively grabbed Kanna's hand as Beppo strode from his chair and placed the box in their hands. Both girls gazed at the strange bird, with its fierce beak and talons, and spectacular colours. As Allarmelu examined the sides, she opened the lid. Now she was in paradise. These were European chocolates, presented to her by a European. The first bite was divine. She swiftly transformed into a goddess, offering the wisdom of that taste to everyone else in the room without being prompted.

Ramulu had cleared the tea trolley with immaculate grace and in silence. Jagan coughed politely and the revelry paused. Ramulu reappeared with a cloth parcel on a large silver tray and waited for Jagan to stand up. Jagan walked from his desk over to Beppo. Dharma fidgeted and uncrossed his legs, and dabbed the perspiration from his forehead with his monogrammed handkerchief as

Jagan passed him. Beppo looked from one brother to the other, not quite knowing what was going to happen.

Allarmelu loved this 'drama' with guests. Presentations. Jagan stood a few feet away from Beppo with his hands clasped, resting on his dignified paunch. To his right and at a distance, marking his place in the presence of his father-like-employer, Ramulu held the tray with the gift. Dharma stood up and this was the cue for Beppo to do the same. Jagan beamed. He took the cloth bag and presented it to Beppo. Allarmelu and Kanna clapped as Beppo received it.

The cloth bag was opened to reveal a shawl. Beppo unfolded it. It was lavender and gold silk, woven in stripes and checks that gave it a double hue. In the centre was a clear square of lavender silk with an embossed sign that looked like a large 'V' with an exclamation mark in between. 'This is the mark of Vishnu. We belong to that sect of Hindus. Krishna leads us. This is from our Tanjore weaver. See, he has even embroidered his name in Tamil here.

'I was told the weaver who created this was inspired by the sunset during the monsoon—so the colour of the gold is almost like copper, and the sky does turn the colour of mother-of-pearl,' added Jagan.

Beppo clearly acknowledged the authority and affection of Jagan. All he could say was: 'I am deeply touched by your welcome, and honoured, Signor Jagan. I feel I am welcomed in the heart of India.'

'You must come again, and also visit our looms in Seeraivakkam, a village close to Tanjore.'

'I'll certainly arrange that. Tell me when you would like to go, Beppo,' Dharma added. The golden tassles gleamed like shark's teeth as he assisted Beppo with folding the shawl into the cloth bag.

Allarmelu could sense the evening was over. It would soon be time for farewells. If only her mother was well enough to come down, then Mr Beppo could see what a real beautiful Indian lady is, she thought. Jagan placed his arm around Dharma, in a gesture of reassurance that as a younger brother he could proudly bring his friend home, and not lurk around clubs all the time.

When the coach carried away the visitors, Allarmelu ran back to her lacquered box. She stroked the golden bird and, hoping Kanna would never find out, opened the box and placed the truffle deep in her mouth. Her saliva dowsed and dissolved it into a sea combed with flavours of chocolate, the sweetness of importance and the crunchiness of differences. She believed she was the lady of the house, of *Surya Vilas* and that was her first experience of ecstasy.

At Home with Courtesans

Beppo was scheduled to attend an official function and was set down at the Railway Hotel to dress formally for the occasion. The strong, greasy aroma of his pomade lingered even after the door was shut. As the air cleared, Dharma felt he was now at the helm, steering a dream into a reality. He was triumphant. Jagan had approved of Beppo, and Beppo was impressed with *Surya Vilas*. Allarmelu was worth that pearl bangle he had given her; she turned out to be such a terrific hostess and entertainer. If it hadn't been for her, he thought, he would have felt as joyless as a tiger dining on diced meat served on a porcelain plate.

The meeting between Jagan and Beppo was a miracle; a stroke of genius on his part. There were innumerable hurdles that could have made the meeting not happen. First, Jagan and Beppo led lives with engagements scheduled in the mornings and evenings. Dharma discovered it wasn't easy inviting a European home. While Jagan did drink alcohol and eat meat, there were certain days that he abstained from both for special religious and traditional practices. Mondays for Shiva, Tuesdays for Hanuman, Thursdays for his family guru, Saturday for Venkatesvara, and sometimes on Friday for Amman—so only Wednesdays and Sundays were a possibility. But then Dharma had agonized, should he invite Beppo for dinner or lunch?

The week after the picnic, Chellamma was ill and confined to her bedroom. She did not respond to his notes asking whether he should invite Beppo for tiffin; he blamed Gowri and Ruku for confiscating them. At last, Dharma had the marvelous idea of High Tea. It was English and Indian. In Madras, High Tea was fairly substantial, with a menu of homemade sweets and sumptuous savouries. It was between two halves of the day, just after an afternoon nap when other appointments would not take place. It need not be official, it could be formally informal, just like the dress code. It was an 'introduction' to two forces that were imperative to Dharma's future. Jagan was the force that came with family wealth and tradition and all that India meant. Beppo, as a European, spurred Dharma's biggest adventure toward freedom and independence from the great force of economic stability that Jagan represented. Dharma knew the meeting was significant in fostering trust between Jagan and Beppo. And that was ensured. Jagan seemed to consider Beppo 'honourable' and Beppo declared what he felt about Jagan's welcome.

The next hurdle was to get the investment for the European tour of the ballet. Dharma had alluded to a vast supply of silk as a donation for the set design of the new ballet. He sensed Beppo's keen eye for sartorial symbolism. Beppo, in turn, was on the hunt for a mysterious motif, religious even, that had never been used before in either Theatre or Dance productions: an oriental geometric design with symbolic references. It would make the forthcoming production unique in the eyes of world audiences, bringing together Russia, India and Europe. This was why Dharma couldn't resist the opportunity that Chellama's pomegranate-pink wedding sari afforded him when it slid into his hands the evening of the picnic. That was daring. A private family ritual and its act of worship during the Pongal harvest would now become a public fact, or so he thought.

The prospect of events unfolding as he had engineered them gave Dharma an erection. The drive, with Beppo glancing time and again at the lavender shawl with its coppery gold tassels, that he kept stroking like he would a lapdog's ears, made Dharma feel assured of his partnership in the next season of the Russian Ballet. He felt in the need of a celebration.

As Dharma sighed with the satisfaction of the many things he had yet to put in place, he decided to meet Lali, his mistress. She would know his comforts, and in any case, the infant, his child, would be asleep by now, so he could have her all to himself. He had now to find a way of telling her, and include her in his plans.

It was dark by the time he arrived at her house in Puraswalkam. Light was dimly streaming from the inner courtyard onto the front verandah, and he could hear the musicians playing a soft and sensuous melody with the veena leading. He stood at the verandah, and then entered another world. Here was the inner courtyard where devotional songs with erotic lyrics were sung by courtesans of the divinities in the Carnatic tradition. After all were not gods and humans lovers? He was welcomed with strands of jasmine, kadamba, the faint scent of tobacco rolled in paan, dusted with desiccated coconut and Johnnie Walker Red Label scotch.

When he entered, the musicians played at a faster tempo. Lali was beating the talam rhythm to her singing with her right hand on her knee. She was seated cross-legged on a mat, her vermillion mark in the centre of her forehead a statement of motherhood, and aspiring consort. The musicians with violin, flute, mridangam leaned forward to keep the thread of her eye contact as she conducted them effortlessly. She acknowledged Dharma's presence with a deferential bow of the head, and the musicians bowed low as they played. He was their financial patron, with family money of course. Then with a flourish of the hand and her head, she ended her last note and the music on perfect timing.

The musicians folded their palms and closed their eyes offering a thanks to the music in the air, and so did she, and then they all bowed to each other. Dharma marveled at their awareness of physical proximity, as they bowed so deeply several times without colliding with either their instruments or each other's heads, in such a confined space. He knew all too well that, for them, the music was a presence. Even if it was ephemeral, in the concert it had held all of them together in spite of the diverse sounds and shapes of the instruments. For now they bade farewell to the music until the next time. Then, and only then, did all of them turn to Dharma.

Servants huddled in and drinks were offered, green sherbet and alcohol. Each one of the musicians dipped their middle fingers and sprinkled the drops on the floor with a prayer. Dharma couldn't help smiling. He had seen them in their various states of intoxication, from mild to extreme. But before entering that realm, they dipped their fingers in the drink and sprinkled it around them as if it were holy water. Each muttered his mantra inaudibly, making the space sacred. It was almost as if they had to invoke the gods to protect them from their demons shortly to be unleashed; to give them sanction to hurtle toward human rawness after creating divine music.

Lali went indoors to feed the baby. Dharma was now a father to a secret daughter, who would carry her mother's tradition of Dasi, or mistress, forward. He watched Lali as she turned her back. Her moves were not as nimble as before. But her weight made her look more authoritative, yet softer. Her jet-black plait accentuated with tassles swung below her hips and swayed when she walked barefoot to the jingle of her silver anklets. The cluster of jasmines enmeshed in her hair exuded their night perfume.

Just before she disappeared into the doorway Lali tossed her head and looked straight at Dharma and then lowered her eyes. She swung her long black plait around to the front and twirled a loose string of jasmine as if it was coming undone—or was she undoing it? The gold pearl-and-ruby-studded bangles clinked around her plump wrists. Her breasts, hips, all seemed fuller. The South African diamonds of the nose studs that he had gifted her on her debut all those years ago flashed. She was in his eyes the real, the mythological, the calendar goddess that he had desired and bejeweled over the years. Her look was an invitation, and his steady stare with a smile curling at his left cheek, an acceptance. He would spend the night with her. It would also be the first time he would be setting eyes on their child. They had the perfect understanding. Guests departed, and the last oil lamp in the upper apartments was snuffed out.

Dharma placed a gold chain around Lali's head, and against her loose hair it glinted like lightning. Her throbbing neck and his sense of accomplishment of the day made them cut to the quick of passion. They were lovers who laughed a lot, and teased each other mercilessly. At last they collapsed into a daze. Dharma was in bliss. In Lali's bed he dreamed of four wives. He was the prince who had created a celestial kingdom in an ordinary forest, as his wives were courtesans descended from paradise. He remembered the story as an aunt would mischeivously tell him about the virtues of a 'disobedient' son.

In his dream it was so clear. His first wife was Indra's daughter. She looked like Lali at first, then turned into Valentina. She had left her sari by the edge of a pond where she began bathing. Unnoticed by her, Dharma picked up a corner of the sari and started running, the sari billowing in the wind. His wife, the heavenly courtesan, ran after him. Unable to catch up, she pleaded with him to return the sari. 'I promise I'll marry you, and as I'm Indra's daughter, you will have all the wealth of the gods, please return that sari to me!' She started singing. It made him stop in his tracks on the open country road with white clouds in a cool morning sky. He stood still and could feel the dry red earth beneath his feet, cool from the night before. He scrunched his toes and looked down. He could feel her breath and lips on his neck as she clasped his hand. When he turned to look she was running ahead of him, wrapping the sari around her, and she started flying toward the clouds.

A dog barked and whined. Dharma opened his eyes. It was dark and Lali's sweat had soaked his jubba. The stale jasmines in the bed began to make his stomach lurch. He gathered his senses. He was not a prince of a celestial kingdom in a forest. But Lali was his courtesan and he would make her his queen. She was so satisfying. The layers of silk that had to be tussled with, the shapes unseen, the sweet stickiness of a newborn's milk, all made the night a celebration fit for a man who was going to make history. The prospect of being a father brought tenderness. Dharma didn't feel he owned Lali now; she had a hold on him. 'Had I married, I would never have felt this way', he sighed. Apart from his brother Jagan, all he saw in marriages around him were much older men married to very young girls who bred children. He couldn't help feeling sorry for women. Their life from birth to death was an unending chronicle of mothering their husbands; their dotage in return for the status of being married women. 'At least I know I love her. And Valentina.' It was still dark, and he would have to leave before the parrots announced the break of day. It was time to get up. He heard the milk cart rattle on the rickety cobbled pathway, with its buffalo mooing as the cock crowed.

There were many tasks to accomplish. Contacting Beppo without delay and going to Tanjavur had to be arranged by the end of the day. If Beppo saw the looms and the silk, Dharma could buy time to get the 'loan' from Jagan to deliver him from this position of negotiating with fantasies. Once he had the money, Beppo had always indicated Dharma would be an equal partner. Totally equal.

Dharma eased himself out of bed, removing Lali's arm that was slung across his chest. It was heavily laden with a yard of the gold bangles that he had presented her over the years. She did not stir, or even let out a snore. He gathered his dhoti and his jacket and slipped out of the room, carrying his socks. He tiptoed down the staircase of the house that he rented for Lali. A blur of early-morning light washed in from the inner courtyard into the hall. He remembered leaving his shoes under the bench by the Georgian doorway. Suddenly, his blood ran cold.

The front door was ajar. He could barely believe what he was seeing. Valentina appeared in a soft lavender muslin dress with a shawl fringed with silk-and-glass-bead tassles. The stray dog began whimpering and barking, hesitant whether she was an intruder or was known to the master. Her voice bristled with anger in spite of her efforts to keep it low: 'Why didn't you tell me? You never told me you had a child!'

Dharma dropped his socks and went toward her. Her tassles were clinking like cut-glass pendants from a chandelier. She was his future, who could soon become his past. He wanted to comfort her. He took one swift move forward and put his hand over her mouth. She scratched him. The copper jug of water on the side table fell and clanked on the stone floor. She was now writhing on the floor, trying to get Dharma's hand away from her mouth. Finally, they both steadied themselves by grabbing at the leg of the table. Dharma tried to restrain her.

'What the hell do you think you are doing here at this time of day?' His voice, close to her ear, held concern, if that could be possible.

'I wanted to know if it's true.' She stood. Her eyes flashed and her breathing was more like hissing. She had walked all the way from Perambur to Puraswalkam and the scrabble on the floor had left her breathless. Neither of them had expected the encounter, and yet they knew they would meet.

They heard a click, repeated. Dharma whirled around. It was Lali standing on the stairway with a Winchester rifle. 'Have you gone mad? Put that down!'

Lali now had her finger on the trigger and straightened the muzzle to aim at Valentina. 'Why should I? She knows why she's here.'

Valentina turned to run, and Lali fired. It hit the Hyderabadi glass chandelier. Valentina screamed and fled, leaving a trail of blood. The dog wailed as it was hit by shrapnel off the chandelier. There was no sign of any servant.

'Where the hell did you get that gun?' Dharma asked once he got his courage back.

Lali stood imperially on the staircase. She looked every bit like Kannagi raging at the King's court, seeking justice. 'I have learned to love the Police too, you know. At least they offer protection. Now get your things, and get out!'

Ending an Era

Madras, March 1910

Allarmelu skipped across the garden of *Surya Vilas* to where Kanna was seated on a sackcloth. She was busy sorting the flowers by size and colour and nothing could distract her. The plucked flowers in tiny heaps around her were like paints on a palette. She combined the colours of orange kannakambaram, yellow marigold, green tulasi leaves into garlands that would be offered during the evening worship at *Surya Vilas*.

Allarmelu wore a white sailor-suit blouse edged with a bright sky-blue border, much like in the portrait of the princesses with the Tsar Nikolai Romanov. Today she felt like an empress and stuck her stomach out. She was trying to include Kanna in her reverie and concluded: 'a full stomach is as round as the whole world. Only a supremely powerful person can carry a full stomach.'

Kanna was wearing a crushed green pavadai skirt and a pink blouse that had once fitted Allarmelu. Allarmelu watched how Kanna's nimble fingers dexterously wove the purple and orange flowers with fragrant leaves into a strand for them to play with. The girls shut their eyes tight and smelled the strand, trying to distinguish which fragrance was more overpowering. They then decided to make a strand as thick as a python and as long as they were tall. But as the thread and flowers wiggled around their bobbing index fingers, it turned into a game of finger puppets. Then another layer of entertainment was added and they made up rhymes, which ended in cackling laughter as they vied with each other as to who was the funniest.

From upstairs in Allarmelu's mother's bedroom, something fell and broke. The girls were oblivious to everything except their absolute glee at coming up with so many different nonsense words that rhymed. Words did not have to have meaning. They understood each other.

Bun, bun!
Yemi bun?
Tea bun? Jam bun?
Ledu! Hair bun
Oho, fun bun a-a!

With the sun, the smell of tender green mangoes was thick in the air as they released their milk. The inner courtyard contained the sun. The drying red chillies and vats of vinegar made one sneeze when the sea breeze clocked in daily at 2 p.m. Now it was 12. Midday. It was the time when girls were not allowed to sit under the shade of the tamarind tree. Spirits came out and possessed them. They must sleep indoors, or else their skins would get black. It wasn't time for lunch yet and the girls were getting hungry with all this headless laughter.

Allarmelu was an only child, in spite of her mother carrying many children. They went straight from the midwives' hands to the cremation ground. The wise old women believed, 'those poor souls cannot enter this kali

yuga world. The world that will end all worlds with its
iron will and greed for money.' The more caring relatives
would make Allarmelu sit on their laps and hold her chin
and affectionately tell her that she was made of sterling
stuff to survive in a world of steel and iron, money and
men.

The gardener Perumal Joseph, a recently converted
Catholic whose several children studied at Presentation
Convent, came running into the garden, wobbling under
the weight of the old railway clock he carried. It usually
hung in the entrance of the courtyard leading out to
the driveway. IMPERIAL TIME was etched across the
cracked cream face of the octagonal dial. Sparrows had
built a nest between the beam and the hook that hung
the clock. This made the sparrows chatter louder over
the ticking of the clock and the needles jumped. It was
decided that no one could keep time by that clock, least
of all the watchman guarding the grounds.

The girls ran to Joseph Perumal and he imperiously
told them how to read the time with the Roman numbers.
It was a bit confusing, as the girls knew their numbers in
Telugu, but these Roman numerals were in Allarmelu's
opinion utterly unnecessary, as no one spoke Roman
in the house let alone counted in it. She and Kanna
determined that the clock would keep the correct time
if the numerals were changed to Telugu. Joseph Perumal
was flabbergasted that the child could actually think of
a world without a European master and sacrilegiously
suggest Telugu numbers replace the Roman ones!'What
is this world coming to! Kali yuga-a!' he muttered in
sheer disbelief. He called on his pantheon of Hindu gods
and Christian saviours:'Madhava! Madhusudana! Mary
Mother! Govinda! St Christopher!'

The girls giggled as he sped off in a huff on his spindly bowlegs, clutching the clock as if he needed to protect this object of time from some turbulent wave of change. He looked like an awkward Father Time puppet, with the clock face larger than his head, held up by his thin arms, bobbing out of the gateposts of *Surya Vilas*.

He merged into the traffic of people on Flowers Road. Women in purdah, servants, and urchins poured in and out of fruit and vegetable market stalls along the road. The neighing of horses and ponies hitched on to all manner of transport, from tonga to coach, resounded. Traffic was at a high point of the day, ferrying lunch to all the officials and clerks in the courts, as well as civil servants in the Grand Post Office. Allarmelu could barely see above the compound wall, but the flurry of activity made her curious about the world outside. She didn't notice the coachman scurry out of the house, on foot, holding a letter from the doctor who was waiting at the front door of the house.

'Allarmelu!' she turned around to see her favourite Doctor Chinnaina and ran to hug him. He knelt down, and held her by her shoulders, and fixing his gaze on her eyes said, '*Amma ni poi chudu, upudu.*' He had instructed her to see her mother immediately. Allarmelu beckoned Kanna and, both of them cradling their pavadais so they wouldn't trip, ran up the stairs to the grand bedroom, giggling.

The day before Allarmelu had been told she would get a present. She thought it might be a new brother or sister all of her own to play with and teach. When she entered the bedroom with the edge of her pavadai in her mouth, she saw her mother lying in bed. While the other attendants greeted the girls with a 'shush!' her mother

only said, 'Come my darlings, come.' She was thinner
than yesterday. Sweat was pouring from her forehead.
Her hair clung to her head like wet black paint.

Allarmelu pulled her pavadai out of her mouth and
with her dancing eyes jumped onto the foot of the bed.
Her mother's firm teak bed and its headboard carved
with a rising sun between two elephants, was brought as
part of her trousseau into Surya Vilas to complement its
name. 'Aiyeee!' the two ayahs chorused disapprovingly,
being protective over their patient. Both aunts stood
like sentinels, clasping their fear like ammunition in
their hands.

'Allallu,' Allarmelu's mother said, stroking her
daughter's feet as she sat cross-legged, and wiggled into
a comfortable position close to her. Kanna stood by the
corner of the bed jingling her tiny bangles. 'Allalu, Amma
has to go for a while. What will you do?'

'Where is Naina taking you? Will there be chocolates
there? Will you bring back lace?' Allarmelu's eyes
brightened.

Her mother intended to laugh, but coughed. A hoarse
and hacking cough that nearly catapulted her out of her
bed. The ayahs swooped and swarmed around her and
one of them gave her a red liquid poured from a clear Polish
cut-glass decanter. Allarmelu was certain this was blood
to drink; she had seen her mother once sitting in a pool
of blood when yet another baby disappeared on arrival.

'Allalu, I've told Naina to bring you lace, and that
music box you wanted. But now you are a big girl…'

'Ammmmma! What does that mean? Everyone says
I'm a "big" girl. I don't know what to do!' Allarmelu
pouted and lay down close to her mother. So thin and
frail, but so much love pouring out from her.

'Why do you say that, my bangaru? All I want is that you look after Naina. Make sure our Kanna is looked after and whatever you get you must share with her.' Allarmelu wondered if Amma was going away to have another baby. She felt her mother's absence every time there was the news that she would soon have a brother or sister. It had been at least nine times that Allarmelu could remember, from since she was four years old.

It was a pattern. Amma would be sitting at the table—in the dining hall, or in Naina's study. Naina's sisters would be with her. Amma had a way of making the atmosphere congenial, even if the women were in territory that exuded male officialdom. It had that scent of wood-framed glass-paneled book cabinets. The French polish mixed with the aroma of sandalwood. When Naina wasn't there, even menus would be planned, as well as discussions about weddings. When the men were in the room, the women took to silence and embroidery. Then there would follow months when her Amma wouldn't be able to go out, and the weeks when she would have to lie in bed.

But there were also months that Allarmelu remembered, when her Amma and Naina would host parties at home or go out for picnics. Amma would be dressed in Tanjavur silks for festivals. When Naina had his Lawyer and Professor friends over, her mother would wear the Parsi glass-bead-bordered saris, and would read Telugu poetry. Amma was slight but always so beautiful. Naina was at least twenty years older, and was a large, generous man. Her Amma had a musical voice, open smile, and sheer grace because the breeze always blew when she walked into a room. Amma's sisters-in-law clung to her for lightness in a world darkened by men.

Surya Vilas was their home and only refuge, and it was fortunate that Amma's delicate health and gentle nature made the three of them care for each other. They were all nearly the same age.

But for Allarmelu, her Amma made world news because she could write poetry, speak in English, and walk confidently in front of Naina when she was allowed to.

'Naina said you were such a good hostess, the day Dharma Chinnaina brought the Italian gentleman.'

'Amma, he wasn't Italian. He was U-rope-ian.' Her mother smiled and began coughing. More blood. More red drink. Allarmelu took the glass from Gowri's hand, cradled her mother's frail neck and cautiously poured the red drink into her mother's mouth. She looked at her mother's eyes wandering at the ceiling. The women huddled closer. Kanna began to cry. Allarmelu felt such a stinging pain in her heart and throat, the like she had never known before. Her mother looked at her.

'You are my Ganga.' A wail from the women as they hushed Chellamma, cautioning her not to speak and to save her dying energy. 'Tell Naina, the sari has gone. Pongal... Please light the lamps...make sure the milk boils over... My mother's sari...her mother's sari...your sari... Dharma never came to see... O mother, Devi! Mahasakthi!' Allarmelu saw the light sink in her mother's eyes. She was fixed cradling her mother and the glass. She felt an electric current pass through her. Her aunts screamed and the ayahs wailed. Kanna prised the glass out of Allarmelu's hand. Allarmelu eased her mother's head on the pillow and watched the eyes so still and inward, yet smiling. She buried her head in her mother's chest and stayed there till the suppleness of the body turned rigid, warm sweat turning cold.

More than Cooking in the Kitchen

By 1 p.m., the news had spread. Jagan hurried breathless upstairs without removing his outdoor shoes and saw his wife and daughter huddled into one silent, immovable sculpture. He tried to pull Allarmelu away. She was the weight of granite. Hardly able to hear himself as his voice was being pressed by the stones in his throat, he muttered, 'Allalu… Amma left us. We are alone now. Allalu, she left before I could come. Allalu…she left us alone, together.'

His sisters were sobbing inconsolably at Chellamma's feet. The Cook and Kanna bayed the way dogs do while escorting the souls of the dead to unseen realms. Jagan's hands and knees were trembling as he sat on the edge of the wide teak bed, alone. Allarmelu still had her head buried in her mother's chest and suddenly shot out her arm and held her father's hand firmly. She sat up. There was a momentary hush. There were no tears staining her face. This was a greater shock for Cook who beat her chest with her fists and screamed. 'Aiyiyo! Cry! Allalu, cry! Don't hold it back! Stay with us Allalu! Don't become a stone!'

And they all wailed. 'Your mother, our beloved Chellamma, may she go to the lap of the gods; she was a goddess on earth. She would never want you to become a stone.' But Allarmelu sat, and looked at them as if *they* were stone, carved into a grotesque manifestation of humans, set in a cloud of gloom.

While she had held her dying mother, Allarmelu had felt a current, a rush of energy like water but as light as fire, and warm. It was only now she understood something her mother had always talked about: the soul, and love. She knew she would always remember that, and she would hold on to it. It made her feel light.

The sari. Her mother remembered it. It was to be worn at the festival. She would have worn it. But it never came back. It seemed like a long time since that picnic, when Dharma took the sari away to darn it. She remembered pressing herself close to her mother then, how alive and well she was then. She also remembered the magical smile that spread across Dharma's face when the sari slid into his hands, the way his promise to return with it mended, reassured his mother on that happy day.

Allarmelu saw her father sitting. A fly sat on his forehead and buzzed back and forth from her mother's head to his. He was breathing, but he seemed as insensate as her mother's body. Tears were streaming down his face, his chin, and drenched his cotton jacket and jubba. He had smeared the Vaishnava caste mark on his forehead, as if to wipe his fate clean and start again. He seemed oblivious to the lament that was sung in the room.

'Chellamma was the sum of love, a million suns across time's seasons creating bountiful harvests; the value of gold; anyone who crossed her doorstep never left the house in hunger; no one felt greedy in her presence; she fed the poor, even the black stone gods in all the temples would smile for her; flowers always adorned her hair; she left this world as a sumangali, a married woman—blessed not to bear a widow's shame; she loved truly till the last; her love will spread like the rays of the sun and rise every morning, undiminished, with the fragrance and uprightness of a lotus, to protect her child and her husband, beyond *Surya Vilas*.'

Allarmelu's was the last face her mother saw before dying. Allarmelu had seen her face reflected in her mother's eyes. She would always remember that…Amma would always be there to look after her. Allarmelu held her father's hand and together, they closed the lids of Chellamma's eyes.

The Doctor came in, and halted with each step he took across the stone floor, not wanting to lift the veil of grief abruptly with practicalities. Allarmelu peeled her father's fingers from the steady grip in which he held her hand. Her legs were shaking as she slid down from the bed. Jagan was still seated on the bed, gazing at her mother, his wife. Standing beside him, she held her father's head, and rested it against her tiny shoulder. His tears fell like rain, and she kept wiping them with her tiny hands and then dried them on her pavadai. Her eyes remained dry.

The Doctor circled his arms around Jagan and Allarmelu. 'She was a great lady,' the Doctor sighed. 'I'm sorry I could not do enough'.

Jagan spoke as if his voice was coming from a deep well. 'It's god's way. You did what you could within your power. There is a greater power that gives and takes life. I hope she can finally rest.'

The Doctor thought it best to mention practicalities

now.'We must now get the women to prepare Chellamma for the final journey. You too must get ready for the last rites. I'll make arrangements for Allarmelu to be with my family…'

Swift as a flyswatter, Allarmelu said, 'No. Thanks Doctor Chinnaina. I want to be with Amma. She told me not to leave Naina, to look after him. Tell him, Naina.' Allarmelu looked at Jagan. This was not an appeal; it was a command.

'But little girls your age must not…' the Doctor tried reasoning.

'I am Naina's daughter! He needs me. I must stay with him. And, I'm not a little girl!'

Jagan, dazed and shocked as he was, saw sense in her defending her right.

The Doctor was persistent, being an old family friend, 'Jagan, we will look after Allarmelu. You know that. After all she has seen, the child needs the attention of a family. She's at an age when…' he stopped suddenly.

Jagan felt life slipping through his fingers. Allarmelu was now standing with her arms akimbo looking at her father. She could see her father waking from his daze, she could almost hear him thinking, 'Doctor means well, but Allarmelu is different.' She remembered how often she heard her aunts and visiting female relatives say to her mother, 'you're spoiling this girl rotten. She has her own ideas about things. She says what she thinks. What will she do in her husband's house? An overripe mango has not many uses. You must tone her down a bit.' And Chellamma, on the days when she and Allarmelu were having a quarrel would, in turn, tell Jagan, 'you spoil her rotten. She says whatever comes into her head.

No respect for authority!' Jagan would respond, 'what authority? Is there colonial rule in this house as well? How will India ever be free if Allalu doesn't speak up!' and they would both laugh.

Jagan's face changed. Allarmelu dropped her arms. Suddenly everything was moving so fast, that she felt she was running, standing in the same spot. Her father stood up steadying himself with the Doctor's support. 'Take Allarmelu with you…but only over my dead body. She will be with me, and grow up in her home, in *Surya Vilas*.'

He turned and walked out of the room. His large frame could not conform to the blow life had just given him. Allarmelu saw Doctor looking crestfallen. She put her arms around his waist and hugged him.

Once the men had left the room, the wailing started again. Allarmelu sat between Gowri and Ruku on the floor at the foot of her mother's bed. Linking their arms together, they were nursing the deep hollow they felt with death of Chellamma. For the unmarried aunts it was also mourning the end of an era of light and happiness. Allarmelu sat counting all the instructions her mother had given, repeating them like a mantra in her head.

An elder female relative, who had been sitting for a while, announced that the deceased had to be washed in turmeric, embalmed, and dressed for the last rites. There was a muttering amongst the female relatives about which sari had to be tied around the body. All of Chellamma's jewellery had to be taken off and carefully presented to Jagan. *Which sari?* Something tore in Allarmelu's heart. Her mother was going to wear the wedding sari for the festival. Now that sari wasn't there, to be placed beside her mother to fulfil her last wish. *Where was that sari?* Allarmelu was fidgeting.

'The child is going to have a fit. Somebody give her a tumbler of Horlicks. She's been through a lot. Let her not fast,' said a great-aunt who had arrived.

'Amma liked red.' When Allarmelu said this, both Gowri and Ruku lifted their heads and looked at each other. The three of them were thinking the same thought. The topic of the wedding sari would definitely come up, as it would need to be placed before the body, customary for a woman who dies a sumangali.

'Yes Allalu, we'll tie the new red one with the temple border,' said Gowri. Allarmelu watched how nimble both her aunts were in hushing the relatives and consoling them while extracting the ring of house keys from under the deceased's pillow.

Women relatives were swarming into the room. As a mark of respect to the dead, none of the women wore jewellery. Some were whispering instructions, '...for twelve days no food must be cooked in this house where death has marked the door'. The younger women who were their daughters-in-law were making arrangements to plan a menu of meals for mourners, as observed in the death rites. For eleven days these meals would be brought in throughout the day from various households to feed *Surya Vilas*. On the twelfth day, 108 orphans, destitutes and widows would be invited for a feast, to liberate the soul of the dead.

The humid air was filled with the smell of cough mixture and sweat, mixed with coconut-oiled hair. Allarmelu made her way to the kitchen in search of

Kanna who had to be taken away as she wailed the loudest, in concert with her mother, Cook.

Allarmelu heard unfamiliar voices coming from the kitchen. She approached and stood in the doorway. Gowri and Ruku were standing like statues along with Cook. Kanna was the only one still whimpering, almost out of the habit from crying for so long and being hungry.

'Lali, what brings you here?' Gowri was gaining control of the situation as much as she was of herself. 'Jagananna will not like this visit; also with so many of the family here...'

'What on earth were you thinking of? If you think this will make a fine impression on Dharma, then I'll have you know he isn't here!' added Ruku. She surprised herself, and Allarmelu gasped at how an adult can sound just like a child. And yet an adult assumed the right to scold a child for not wanting to share a toy or play with other children.

Lali looked at Allarmelu standing in the doorway and said, 'your mother was always so gracious to me. When I heard she was ill, I thought I'd wait till she got better. I came to have her bless my baby girl. Unfortunately I've come too late. I've named my daughter Chellamma.'

Gowri and Ruku had effectively made themselves extinct. Allarmelu had not seen an infant. While she was curious, she was aware that her aunts, after her parents, had the authority to tell her what to do and not to do, in front of strangers. But the infant was named Chellamma. The name is life, otherwise why were people given names? She knew her mother would be around in one form or another.

'Here, come and hold her Allarmelu.' Lali held out

the infant. The largeness of the black kartikai dot on the forehead of the infant, to ward off the eye of envy from passers by, startled Allarmelu and she looked straight at Lali.

'How do you know Dharma Chinnaina?

Ruku bunched her shoulders, wrinkled her nose and stared with great determination at the red stone floor as if it would give the right answer. Gowri folded her arms, pouted and rolled her eyes and stared at the teak beams of the kitchen ceiling as if she had never seen it before in all her years of growing up in *Surya Vilas*.

'You can say we are known to your family for a very long time, long before you were born,' Lali said as she wiped a tear with a handkerchief that she pulled out from her blouse. The infant stirred. Allarmelu walked up to Lali, who handed her the naked infant. Allarmelu had never known anything as soft. She had only known her mother's skin to be this soft, as she bathed with ground green gram flour and Pears soap. The infant smelt of rose water. Just as Allarmelu rubbed her nose against little Chellamma's cheek, a little spout of urine dribbled down her sailor suit. The women laughed and quickly covered their mouths to stop the jollity, which could be misunderstood in a house of mourning. Gowri and Ruku quickly recovered the infant from being dropped by Allarmelu's instant disgust as she flicked the urine off her suit.

'Go and change out of that and wear your white cotton pavadai sokai, Allarmelu. The water in the boiler is still hot from the morning. Ask Cook to bathe you again, quickly, no talcum powder please!' Gowri was giving instructions. Ruku was rocking the infant while Lali wiped her dry.

Allarmelu left the kitchen but stood in the passageway. She could overhear the hushed conversation.

'He's found another woman. One of those Russian dancers,' Lali began.

'What's that to us? And is this the time you find to announce it?' Ruku was speaking between her teeth.

'If you must know, what I told the child is the truth. I swear on my dance teacher's name. I came to see Chellamma Amma and take her blessings for the baby. Dharma didn't seem to know how ill she was when he came the other night...' Lali had taken the squealing infant back and silenced her with her breast.

'Sssshhh!' Gowri and Ruku were fierce about denying, even to the walls of *Surya Vilas*'s kitchen, Dharma's visits to his mistress.

'Suit yourselves. Block your ears and eyes. That woman will ruin him.'

Gowri said, 'It's really none of our business. It is a man's world.'

'OK. But it's women who make that world turn around.' Lali's impatience with these well-brought-up women, who were perfectly useless in today's world, made her click her tongue derisively. She could even see why Dharma thought they were as prehistoric as crocodiles.

'Speak plainly. Have you come for money?' Ruku said.

'If that's what I wanted, then I could have shouted from the roof tops of the houses that this baby is Dharma's!'

'Ssshhhhhh!' chorused the sisters again.

'Be thankful I have rescued him from that half-naked Russi woman. Calls herself a dancer! Hmmph! I'll see how long she can stretch and spread her legs!'

'What do you mean?' Gowri was flabbergasted, and Ruku speechless.

'The sari. I rescued it.'

'How on earth....' Ruku was sliding to the floor.

'Whatever happens, don't sack Kuppu,' Lali said, as she left from the back door.

Allarmelu stood fixed in the passageway. She remembered Kuppu was the gardener, Joseph Perumal's, brother. He helped at the celebrations at *Surya Vilas*. He had caught the crabs at the Elliot's Beach picnic with his bare hands and cooked them. Everybody, including Dharma, had commented on the excellent catch of fresh meat.

Pulling Rank

Everyone who turned out at the twelfth-day ceremony for the ascension of Chellamma's soul—and they turned out in hundreds—saw a change in *Surya Vilas*. The procession shuffled along the carriage driveway from the gatepost till the stables. Men in twos or threes and women and children in groups of seven. Chellamma had touched many lives, which could fill a local ethnographic survey. There were vegetable sellers, temple lepers, flower girls, sweepers, Muslim and Hindu cooks. There were aristocrats who travelled from Hyderabad and the royal houses of Orissa, as well as Madras University professors and students, and impoverished musicians and dancers whom she saw fit to sponsor at temple festivals. There were villagers from her parents' home in Tanjavur who had come on foot and by bullock cart, as well as families from the seven hills of the Tirupathi temple.

Jagan had booked temples dedicated to Shiva, Vishnu, Amman and Ganesha in the four cardinal directions of Madras to feed orphans and widows. The carriageway had chatram or palmyra-thatched shelters, for all arrivals to be fed and housed. There were wood fires heating copper vats of water. Rice was constantly on the boil, along with sambar and three vegetables. The rasam of tamarind water was stirred and poured into buckets for serving with deep ladles, followed by cooling curd rice. At death ceremonies such as this one, everyone was vegetarian. Everyone was fed regardless of their caste or creed at *Surya Vilas*.

'A shadow is cast over the brightness of *Surya Vilas*. May she return in a benign form to our world', people muttered and many nodded their heads in disbelief that Chellamma, who gave so generously, should be snatched away from life so soon.

Dharma suffered heartbreak. He could not bear the wailing of the relatives and the waves of unknown people who had changed the face of *Surya Vilas*, so he wept silently in the bathroom. Gowri and Ruku, who had tided over the surge of arrivals by making themselves useful with arrangements for bathing and cooking, could not understand why Dharma took even longer in the bath than usual and hissed at him when he peered cautiously from the door before stepping out in his wet towel.

None of the siblings were wise enough to discover that if had they recounted the incidents in which Chellamma had built bridges of affection in their lives, they might have found some relief from the shock of her sudden absence. 'But anger is all I feel toward them,' Dharma said to himself in resignation. Gowri and Ruku's physical forms repelled him and their wretched state, had Chellamma not saved them, welled up inside him as a cautionary tale—*destitution is an open doorway that knows no difference between rich or poor, man or woman*, he found himself muttering. Their busyness disarmed him and he watched Jagan take them more into his confidence over the arrangements for the cremation and rituals. This was especially marked by Chellamma's absence, as she was the only one who negotiated his inclusion into family discussions. Dharma felt a pariah.

To console himself, Dharma looked in Chellamma's library and found 'Ode to a Grecian Urn' which he remembered reading to her when he studied it for his BA Honours.

'You really love poetry don't you, Dharma?' How quickly she had read his enthusiasm. But Jagan had walked into the library almost bellowing, 'Poetry is good for the soul, but when is this fellow going to take the business forward, eh? Even if he could learn languages—German, Italian—that would help!'

How Dharma wished he had read to Chellamma in her fading hours. She always said his voice understood the effect of words on people. The tears prickled as they rolled down his unshaven cheek, and he bit his lip. He dared not cry in front of the others. He suddenly thought how helpful to his own purposes it would have been to read to her; that way he could have slipped in the idea of the money for Beppo, the silk and the symbols on the sari for the touring ballet. Everything was happening so fast that he could not find the time even to trade her wedding sari. *Where was it now*, he wondered.

The bathroom roof was tiled, with a skylight in the centre. A crow was bashing its beak at the strand of sun bouncing off the metal lining of the glass pane. It brought Dharma to his senses. He shooed the crow away and returned to his predicament. Chellamma had gone. He had organized a trip for Beppo to travel to Tanjavur to visit the weavers' village where temple saris were woven. That was neither here nor there. Suddenly, another thought rippled through his mind. He felt a burning sensation in his groin. He blinked in the bathroom mirror. He looked down and placed his shaving mirror closer to the part, to discover he had a rash around his testicles. His arm shot out for the vial filled with coconut oil and immediately started smoothing it, clinically, so he would not get an erection. It cooled the burning sensation.

But the thoughts that rushed through his head were: What were Lali's connections with the police? All these years he had been maintaining her, her relatives and musicians. He had never suspected, or had reason to believe that there was anyone else who could be master of 'his realm' while he was away. He could walk in at anytime without warning and stay or leave as he pleased. But she had asked him to leave that morning. How dare she. He knew he had to be more authoritative—these courtesans and their games. How harsh she had sounded, and what a fool he had felt, being spoken to like that in front of the retreating Valentina.

Ah! Valentina, he thought. She had come at such a precarious hour, walked all the way from Perambur to see him. *How she must love him*, he consoled himself. It was invaluable for his self-esteem, especially when Lali had diminished him that morning. He suddenly felt a great urge to get out of this traditional household and the indistinguishable multitudes currently thronging it. He was desperate to meet his foreign friends. He craved for that swirling sensation when he was in a world that was so alien to this one. It gave him the exhilarating sense that he might have the chance of discovering who he really was.

He had taken part in the rites of the twelfth-day ceremony. It was time to kiss the dead goodbye and keep her memory alive. When the corridor turned silent, he stuck his head out between the doors. This time he had worn his dhoti and jubba and wrapped a large cotton shawl around his shoulders. He crept toward the narrow stairway to where the stair led down from the upper apartments directly to the kitchen. Cook was blowing through the iron funnel to get the cooking fire started, now that the twelve days of official mourning had passed. The kitchen was filling with smoke and her coughing was loud enough for him to slip past unnoticed to the outside door. He darted out and backed in again. It was Kuppu, with a wicker basket of vegetables on his head, and a large fishnet sack of red onions slung round his wrist with a jute rope.

Kuppu read Dharma's desperation in an instant. He decanted the vegetables into an empty basket on the floor. Dharma stood so close to him that they walked out like man and shadow, Kuppu with basket on head and the flat, empty sack around his shoulders like a cape to camouflage his master. The mourners who were entering *Surya Vilas* didn't notice the two, despite their moving in the opposite direction, as most of them were shuffling along with their eyes cast down in respect.

Perfect timing. By the time they reached the gatepost of *Surya Vilas*, a tonga stood outside with its driver looking for custom, noticing such a stream of people. Kuppu gestured money to the driver with the flick of his thumb and forefinger as Dharma got in, relieved to note he was the sole passenger.

When Dharma got to his apartment, he saw an invitation to the Ace Club from Beppo. *Thank god!* Dharma thought, he managed to wriggle out of *Surya Vilas* just in time to see this. *Gold dust again.*

He wore his western-style suit and looked the part when he arrived. The lights were being lit at the Club's main hall and the wide semi-circular verandah had glass-domed candles winking as the night grew black and humid. Several gentlemen were talking softly, so it meant that tonight there might be ladies present. The atmosphere was tame, yet laced with promise. Just as he crossed the verandah entering the hallway, he heard women's voices. The first door to the left of the Ballroom opened, and he saw Valentina sitting at a table between a middle-aged English gentleman and an English lady who had creases of talcum lining the three folds of her neck, creating the optical illusion of some prosperity: the viewer could not distinguish the talcum from her mounted collar of strands of pearls.

The gentleman looked old enough to be Valentina's father, with flourishing whiskers that flowed into his sideburns, or perhaps the other way around. He was in military uniform and had a surprisingly kind aspect to him, created by the wrinkles around the bags of his eyes.

Valentina wore a green chiffon dress with sapphire and white stone gems that shimmered with the halo from the table lamp. Her right hand was resting at the edge of the card table and was bandaged in a figure eight across her thumb and the palm of her hand. Dharma's heart jumped. Had she sprained her wrist? She saw him, and her breathing gathered pace as the glass beads and sequins on the bodice of her dress twinkled in agitation. Terror froze Dharma on the spot. Her lips parted and in the mellow light he couldn't make out whether she was smiling or mocking, or teasing. He was being held to ransom. Why had he not stayed in the comfort of his grieving family?

Valentina looked enticingly beautiful, and she wasn't even dancing. The gentleman beside her must have caught the change in atmosphere as her perfume seemed to be stronger. Her eyes darted to him and then they both looked at Dharma who was darkening with dread.

'Ah! Signor Dharma!' It was Beppo, entering through the shadows from the left. He winked as he stretched out his arm and patted Dharma on his shoulder. His pomade made his hair look like a slab of dark, glistening chocolate. Dharma nearly jumped, but swiftly recovered himself. Between the pools of light and shadow, Beppo muttered something that Dharma could not catch. In the halo of light now facing Dharma was another Indian gentleman in police uniform.

'So sorry to hear of your sister-in-law's passing away, and so suddenly,' he said. Dharma's forehead was wet with perspiration, turning his ebony curls into wisps of smoke. The police gentleman gave him a monogrammed handkerchief. 'It's the grief. Catches one at any time. Please convey my deepest condolences to your brother; such a grand man.' Between Dharma's terror and the police gentleman's position in front of the light, it seemed impossible to make out his features. It was his gravelly voice, and the rising odour of excessive rice starch as the humidity softened the creases of his uniform that made an impression on Dharma.

'Gentlemen! Introductions! We can't be kept waiting, feeling like strangers in our own company!' said the whiskered English gentleman next to Valentina convivially. His smile showed a gap between his front teeth, camouflaged by his drooping whiskers. Beppo, the police gentleman and Dharma moved in decorous formation to apologise to the company.

'What a sight for sore eyes—an impeccably dressed Italian, a handsome Indian, and an Indian Police Officer!' said the lady sitting by Valentina.

'Colonel Skimore,' said the Englishman as he stood up and shook hands with Dharma. Dharma deftly bowed to the lady, realizing she must be Mrs Skimore, and decided to take a step forward to kiss her outstretched hand. He then looked directly at Valentina and one of his ebony curls fell forward on his forehead as he took her bandaged hand, 'Miss Valentina, I'm deeply sorry to have missed your concert. My family is in mourning.' Everyone looked on. The chemistry was unmistakable and Dharma had declared his winning hand. The police gentleman seemed to sigh at the revelation that they had met before.

Colonel Skimore ordered drinks for the company. The turbaned waiters in their white uniforms flitted across the wooden floor on bare feet, so that the members' conversations would not be impeded by the servers. Mrs Skimore was quick to catch the tone of Valentina's intake of breath. She looked at Dharma with a wistful smile, possibly remembering her own youth and its amorous encounters. 'O dear ! What a pity you missed the concert! A tour de force my dear, absolute tour de force!' Her husband the Colonel who was standing, bowed and whispered in her 'good' left ear. She held her monocle to inspect Dharma even closer for an authentic trace of grief. She was convinced. 'O, I am sorry my dear. Death. Yes. Yes, of course I understand. But it *was* the last.'

Still in mourning, Dharma looked confused. 'O! I mean Valentina. It was her last concert in Madras. She's off to Europe for the season.' Mrs Skimore had an urgency in her tone as if she knew more than she showed, or perhaps it was the Samaritan in her to rescue lovers from loss?

Dharma held his eyebrows high. The black pupils in his melting brown eyes reduced to pin points. He continued smiling while his heart sank to his feet. He could feel the stare of the police gentleman. Is that what Valentina came to tell him at Lali's house? She couldn't leave now! He had to go too, but how?

The evening's events were measured. The band played, people conversed in the intervals, and Valentina continued to ignore Dharma, despite positioning herself so that he could have her in full view from anywhere across the rectangular room. There were some Indian businessmen whom Dharma knew, and he decided to represent his family socially. Having done the full circle like a well-rehearsed script, he and the Colonel happened to catch each other's eye. It had dawned on Dharma while he was circulating across the room, that the colours of Colonel Skimore's uniform were exceedingly familiar.

Dharma ordered an array of drinks and invited Beppo and the police gentleman to join in raising a toast to Colonel Skimore's new post as Surgeon General at Madras. Mrs Skimore recounted more regimental history while the Colonel blushed. Valentina, who was their guest, drew out her hand fan. She acknowledged Dharma's toast as her grey eyes opened wide above the Chinese embroidery of the fan. She unfurled it to reveal crimson silk birds in flight, and began to wave it to cool the animated Mrs Skimore and herself. 'The

80th Carnatic Regiment—what I loved about it were the colours, and it's like coming home—to the Carnatic coast!' concluded Mrs Skimore.

'My great Uncle served at the time when they were forming the Regiment...as a sort of Medical Aide,' Dharma began with a mellow wave of confidence. 'He knew how to cure the Company of snakebite and even found a way of curing the opium bait of the Thugees.'

'Good Gawd!' the Colonel's eyebrows flew up into his hairline. 'I thought I saw a resemblance to the portrait at the Regimental Officers' Mess! L.S. Naidu is your ancestor?! Hmm… He was given a posthumous citation by Her Majesty. His services were commended for the cure. Otherwise, we'd have had more casualties from intoxicants, hallucinations and snakebite rather than fighting the Mutiny! Well, well, well! From the records it shows he died of cholera while visiting an excavation at a temple...Choultry? Such a shame!'

'Ah! but what better place could his soul find rest!' said Dharma with some effect. He wasn't contradicted, as everyone knew he was coming from a house of mourning, and that grief was his currency for the moment.

'Well then, you must receive the citation as a living member of the deceased's family! We *must* get you to England, my dear.' It was Mrs Skimore whose eyes were glittering with excitement as she announced this.

It was the first time Valentina looked at Dharma directly. He felt her captive gaze on him. He was, of course, paying total attention to Mrs Skimore.

Ypres, 1914

A torn broadsheet flapped on the sandbag. The long-expired announcement read:

Stravinsky's Rites of Spring premiered on the eve of the Great War—the listener was confronted with a powerful and frightening spectacle of human sacrifice.

The newspaper had escaped the exchange of gunfire across the trenches and was now rustling in the wind.

Dharma woke to the smell of cordite in the freezing air. He knew where he was and listened with intent to the hum in his head:

No wings on trees
No birds with leaves

The sentence kept writing itself in his inner eye, repeating itself in the inner ear. He realized he had developed these inner organs after arriving at Southampton; as everything was so different from what he knew, these inner beings talked to him more than people did. Was it the voice of his ancestors? He had never taken it seriously when he'd heard his toothless great-aunt telling him of these beings that protected her from famine and arson. He had never known life on the edge, in the raw, and never listened to women's stories, because they could not read or write. So where was the reality in that? He had never seen his mother, but had got into the habit of thinking she looked after him; an always-open door from which he could escape when trapped. Or maybe he really was his ancestor L.S. Naidu, returning from the Mutiny to ease the passage of reincarnated soldiers in these trenches.... He had to bite his lip to pull himself out of this furrow of thinking.

He remembered orders constantly barked, with slaps of rifles, stomping boots and smacking salutes; that's what he saw of England after his arrival, before he was dispatched to offer his services at the Western Front. Just the sound of it in his head made him wake from a surreal no-man's-land of life and death.

Wings, birds, leaves, trees... and yet the logic of sequence made less sense with what was around him. The shock was the reality of the unreal. He kept hearing that this season he was in was 'Spring'. How different English poetry appeared when he had read about it in the season of mango blossom across oceans.

He was shielded in his trench by open guts dripping with congealing blood, like the slaughtered meat he had seen in the larder when he had been taken for inspection at the Regimental Mess. He wiggled his hips to shift the weight of the dead soldier on top of him, but held on to him in an embrace. He could see the reflection of the bare branches in the dead man's eyes. Dharma trembled, closing the unblinking lids. He muttered, 'the last words you must have screamed were *take cover*, Om, Amen.' He slid the body onto a makeshift ledge made from the toppled gun carriage. The bitterness of this cold gnawed at his toes, in turn reminding him he was alive, making him wish he was dead. The coarse woollen socks felt like bandages in his boots. Everything was soaked in blood.

The power and glory of his uniform which was his passport on the voyage from India, and then across the English Channel, chimed with meaninglessness and waste—he couldn't tell which was worse under the concrete grey ceiling of the sky. He must have passed out during the sound of pounding cannon and terrified horses and stuttering gunfire, with hoarse voices in English dialects rising above the rest. On his feet now, he took a cautious look over the snaky trenches lined with sandbags and toppled machine guns.

What in heaven's name, or hell's, was he doing here? His inner conversation began. Was this the journey his namesake Dharma—the God of Right Action—was taking him through? In that Great War, the Mahabharata, with 18 million dead, Yuddhishthira the King of the Pandavas, rides in a chariot along purgatory, with a dog accompanying him. What had Vyasa, the epic poet, said? Yuddhishthira is denied entrance to heaven because he wants a pariah dog to come with him. Yuddhishthira forsakes his entrance because only this dog has loyally accompanied him through all the fogs of illusions, past his body's sheath. When Yuddhishthira clicks the chariot door shut, his feet firmly on earth with the dog beside him, suddenly the dog transforms into the god Dharma.

Stuck in the belly of this trench, with feet in a mud that was constantly dragging him down, he muttered, 'Maya'. What was he doing here without a single qualification except his desire? Valentina's heart had wrapped around him with love and her art had enticed him. It was a romantic dream. He could now taste the sickening cold saliva of loneliness. She was lonely and now he understood the vast loneliness of the Russian landscape she flailed her arms and legs to escape, searching for something to belong to—a spinning ballerina in a paperweight, trapped eternally.

He had had everything around him in Madras, but could not see it. Something drew him to this other life. Was it the privilege of seeing where this foreign empire began, that he wanted to belong to a race that had authority? He realized he was naive in thinking he would belong in a land of poets and Shakespeare. In this fight 'Tommy' did not have enough soup or bread to contemplate the bygone heroism of Lord Byron fighting for the Greeks. Dharma vomited.

Then, clearing his throat, he pulled at his hip flask and rinsed and glugged some brandy down. Pulling out his whistle, he blew it, among the awakening cries of horror from men who had discovered the loss of limbs, or seen those that were blasted off and lay within reach. Dharma bent to pull out the two other men who stirred in the red porridge-like mud.

Attainment

Madras, April 1915

April was the month of prickly heat. It was known as Kathri, the scissor season, as it shredded every human endeavour before it could reach completion. Rich or poor, the human body was paralyzed by the lassitude of this dreaded season's burning heat and high humidity. The thick gold necklaces worn by married women became ropes of fire and their skin puckered into weeping blisters. Talcum and sandalwood paste made good business in European and Indian households as the only fragranced powder that blotted the skin dry. It was not uncommon to see men, women and children plastering their bodies with these substances, making them look like ashen ascetics or actors in a masque, depending on the colour of their skin. Traditional methods of grinding turmeric pods and applying the paste on the skin continued in the women's quarters, resulting in a bright marigold complexion, preferred by some, averse to others.

The Delhi Durbar of 1911 fuelled the relish for talk. Opinions were divided between the wealth of the few and their spectacular display of India, and the waste of their extravagance on colonial guests who never smiled. However, what caught everyone's attention was the presentation of a southern silk sari to the Emperor 'Durbarpet', named so after the sari. It was the talk at the tobacconists, the coffee grinders, the flower sellers and even the Clubs. It was created by a weaver in Madras.

Early this year there were signs in literary circles that India would have its first Nobel Laureate for Literature in English. These developments were considered extraordinary by foreigners and educated Indians; shock was rippling through the world.

Gowri was reading the headlines of the *Evening Telegraph*. Three years ago, the world's mercantile masterpiece made in Britain, the *Titanic*, had hit an iceberg, causing the death of 1,514 men, women and children aboard. In the following year, a German ship, the *Imperator*, rivalling the *Titanic* by an additional 44 feet of steel was fitted with a bronze eagle figurehead, created by Professor Bruno Kruse of Berlin. She carried a banner emblazoned with the motto *Mein Feld ist die Welt* (My field is the world).

Gowri was trying to understand the scale of the world from an artist's image of the *Titanic's* disaster that had been printed on the front page. The world's largest ocean liner was shown bow-end in the waves, with the other part almost in the air; a top-heavy toy boat, nose-diving in a bath. Gowri was wondering whether she might use the word 'titanic' to illustrate a particular event that had occurred in the women's apartments.

It had happened that morning. Allarmelu summoned Ruku and Gowri to examine the sticky patch of blood staining her white bed sheet. Allarmelu saw her aunts' faces contort in horror, disgust, delight, compassion, even secrecy, as they announced their verdict: Allarmelu had 'commenced menstruation'.

Ruku chucked Allarmelu under the chin, and with a girlish grin exposing all her betel-stained teeth, said, 'Allarmelu, you are not a little girl or a big girl anymore. You are a *woman* now!'

Gowri had that adjudicator-at-an-elocution-contest look on her face. When she spoke, Allarmelu couldn't help feeling that it sounded like an announcement her aunt would read from *The Madras Standard*. 'Allarmelu Mangathai of *Surya Vilas*! In this fifteenth year of your life, you are no longer a little girl. You are more than a big girl; in fact, you are now a fully functioning woman. You have Attained Puberty.'

Within that hour, Allarmelu overheard the two sisters chorus to her father who had just completed his prayers in the dining room, 'your daughter is a woman now. She has attained puberty.'

A little later that morning, Allarmelu was nursing her stomach cramps with a hot water bottle wrapped in fine muslin as she lay on the chaise longue in Jagan's study. Since she was mistress of the house, and as yet unmarried, the conventional regime of confinement to the women's apartments during menstruation had not yet been suggested. Everyone knew that it would cause a titanic outburst at *Surya Vilas*.

Allarmelu had no one her age now. Kanna had been sent away by her parents to their village to live with her widowed aunt and tend to their goats and cow. For Cook and her husband Ramulu, this guaranteed protection from the distractions that *Surya Vilas* offered, with so many manservants, and a young girl about to go 'on heat.'

Allarmelu was not going to let her world fall apart or fade away. She argued that if she was beyond a big girl, in fact had been promoted to being a woman by this newly achieved status of 'attaining puberty', who in hell, or heaven, or indeed Hindustan, was going to restrict her movements in the house she lived in, and owned, by her father's admission? Both Gowri and Ruku decided it was best to wait, watch and then say 'I told you so' to whomsoever may dare confront Allarmelu with the ideas of impurity or confinement that were attached to women in their menstruation; 'whomsoever' might have their tongue cut out.

Allarmelu was looking out through the French windows at Joseph Perumal watering the *Tradescantia* border. In April, by 8 a.m. the sun was searing hot, and the perennials were parched. The mango flowers sprayed their scent of anticipation.

Allarmelu saw her father look at Gowri and Ruku standing in front of him. He looked at himself in the mirror in his study. While the gilt-framed mirror was dusted every day, the glass was now streaked with specks of grey. His digestive system was inconsistent after Chellama's death, and there were days when his stomach appeared bloated, and other days when he looked lean and weak. She had administered his diet according to his fasts and feasts, with discretion.

Allarmelu could sense change ripple, not just in her body, but also in the cosmic dance of the household. She could read her father's thoughts; as much as he needed his daughter's intelligent company around the house, two spinster aunts who were an echo of an era of dependence were not going to be enlivening influences for her.

In the years that had passed since Chellamma's death, Allarmelu had taken charge of the household, creating daily menus, distributing gifts to relatives, servants, temples, and priests according to seasonal and religious festivals as her mother used to. All these were central to her role as mistress of the house. The English and French governesses who were brought in to teach her English, French and German, piano, elocution and etiquette were repeatedly replaced within weeks.

When her father insisted that she must have a well-rounded education, she would argue: 'Why? I read the *Iramavtaram*; I sing and listen to Thyagaraja's kirtanas. Look at Andal, she was a woman, what poetry!' Jagan pleaded with folded hands at Allarmelu's frequent outbursts advocating Telugu and Tamil Literature.

'Allalu! You must read Bronte, Austen, Dickens!'

'It's so dispiriting! It's about orphans and cruel people who want their money, and it's always cold! I am sick of reading about people as if they are objects. I want to know about what happens inside a person. Our heroes and heroines also suffer pain, but they dream, with song—and dance! Naina, please, I want colourful stories, stories with life, about our way of life! These women will only teach me "Butler" English!'

She knew by now that Indians would always be subservient to Europeans, and would only ever rise to the status of a butler. She saw this with her governesses. She could not understand their superior attitude in spite of being paid by her father to do a job. Jagan would indulge his daughter with chocolates and she would eat boxfuls and sit in the toilet while the governesses' patience wore threadbare in the heat. Gowri was the only one who made great progress with her confidence in reading the *Madras Times* and *Indian Ladies' Magazine* aloud, in a tone as flat as the inconsequential items she had selected to read out: classified advertisements about knitting needles, gloves,

hand fans and pill boxes available as items for donation to
a Charity of Hindu widows, who had recently converted
to Christianity.

Ruku would stoically repeat every other hour that all
the reading in the world would not save a woman from
the nausea and crippling pain of menstrual cramps.
Without recourse to anything that could kill the pain, she
would exhaust herself into sleep by vomiting, and hence
the confinement during menstruation to a darkened room
was deemed by her to be a blessing and a comfort.

In a couple of months, the season of Aadi would arrive.
It was the season when Hindu women fasted and prayed
for their husbands and their families. For Allarmelu, and
for young women like her, a ceremony would be held to
announce to the world that a girl had 'attained puberty',
simultaneously signifying she was ready for marriage.
It was done through a ritual celebrating her entering
'womanhood'.

The ceremony also marked the lunar calendar of a
woman's fertility, or indeed the days when her behaviour
would be affected by the moon. Allarmelu remembered
how her mother and her aunts would stay away from
some foods. It was a way of detecting when the cycle
was approaching. Pickles in particular and coconuts
were left out of reach of all women in the household and
visits to the temple were not allowed. She remembered
Cook recounting when she went to the temple during
her periods and, completely forgetting about it, offered
a coconut at the shrine. 'When it was split open, the
priest gave me such a scolding! I saw it, Allalu, inside it
was all black and rotten because I touched the coconut
when I was in my period.' If Cook had tried forewarning
Allarmelu about the period and how it shackled

every woman into submission, then it certainly fell on deaf ears.

Allarmelu remembered the day her mother died. After Lali had left from the kitchen and the back door, Dharma arrived from the verandah. Allarmelu had never seen him so distraught. Jagan had to console him. Dharma kept muttering, 'There will never be anyone like her...' and he wept. All through the time that Gowri and Ruku were dressing the body, Allarmelu heard her Chinnaina sighing and crying in the corridor saying aloud, 'O! What is to become of us! She is gone, the light from our lives is taken away!'

For the next few months he came to the house every week, unshaven. The day his beard seemed to be trimmed, he suddenly announced that he was going to Europe. He muttered unconvincingly about being back for the first-year anniversary of Chellamma's death. Jagan looked ashen as his brother left in the carriage, knowing full well that he might not return.

Allarmelu saw her father looking lost and without hope for the first time. He explained to her that his company's exports to Germany were not successful. The price of salt all across India was increasing. Jagan felt it was a travesty for a people who never had to pay for salt as it 'was of the earth, and of this blood'. That a tax had been levied by the British government on Indians making salt from its vast coastlines was met with even greater horror, and suffering. Only salt from Cheshire was to be used. If any Indian was caught using Indian salt, there would be imprisonment for the violation of the government's decree. This had serious implications on Jagan's business of tanning of hides and preservation of reptile shells.

Allarmelu could see her father's health failing, but most importantly, how much he missed the companionship of Chellamma. Allarmelu could not understand why Dharma would leave her father's side at a moment when he was most needed. She found him cruel.

In November, at the height of monsoon, Allarmelu had seen Dharma from the landing of the staircase where she was standing to adjust the portrait of an illustrious ancestor that had tilted. Dharma had come into the hallway with a dripping black umbrella, his jacket and dhoti clinging to his body, smelling of damp and dog fur. He was clutching a cloth bag he had managed to keep dry.

As she had looked down at him, he had looked up, 'I was passing through. Just wanted to hand this over before I leave. It's a pity it's too late. Forgive me.' He had left the bag on the round marble table in the hallway. 'I must go and administer the packing and get things ready for my journey. It will be very cold there.'

Allarmelu had recognized the bag, which had Buckingham and Coromandel Mills printed on it. It was the same bag she had seen him place her mother's sari in—the one that had to be darned. Her aunts and she looked at each other. Allarmelu grabbed the bag; she could see the tassles from the sari, and its pomegranate colour. She had hugged it and wept. Her aunts had hugged her and wept.

This one drop of menstrual blood in the April of 1915 sent a shock of realization that time past was time that could never be recovered, except with the warmth of memory. So many seasons of childhood and its freedoms had flown past with Kanna's departure. Allarmelu clung to the painted box that Beppo had given the two girls. That unforgotten aroma of chocolate reminded her of the first taste of importance, and difference. Above all, it made her ache for Kanna's trusting love. On the day of her leaving, Kanna had plaited a yellow, purple and white ribbon the way she would the strands of flowers. She drew Allarmelu's right hand to her, opened and pressed the plaited ribbons into it. 'These will always be fresh Allalu. I'm always with you the way Amma said we would be.'

Surya Vilas had become a house of silences and grown-ups. However, with the ceremony there was the hope of festivity. For most girls, it was a time when mothers would initiate their daughters into the rite of passage of the 'householder'. But here Allarmelu was at once handling the finances, the staff and her own burgeoning body for a ceremony she felt she had grown out of. But rituals were important. It was theatre, and Allarmelu loved a production.

A month ahead, Allarmelu unlocked the almira that held all the silver containers and gold vessels that had to be laid out in front of the altar for the ceremony. She knew which trays were to be used by the priest for the homa fire and the ones to display the sets of jewellery, the bananas, the betel nut and leaves, and gifts for the guests, the strands of flowers, the coconuts and more.

She opened the safe and took out the sari that had not been removed from the Buckingham and Coromandel Mills bag that Dharma had brought it in so long ago. She couldn't help thinking that the elephant trunk of Ganesha bridged the past with the present. The sari that belonged to her mother, her mother's mother, and was worn by her mother before that. All she wanted now was not a long chain of dead mothers, but her mother, alive. Nothing could replace that. She still remembered the warm current that flowed through her, as she lay still holding on to her mother's frail form. She cradled the bag, reliving the moment she gave her mother that red drink. She breathed deep into the sari, hoping for a waft of her mother's musk.

But this sari did not have the embalming smell of sandalwood and frankincense mixed with turmeric. Allarmelu pulled out the sari from the bag with Ganesha's head and unfolded it. Placing it on her lap, she looked at it, then ran her fingers through the entire nine yards of crinkled gold border. There was no sign of darning. Her heart skipped a beat. When she opened the pallu, she saw all the recognizable symbols of Amman woven into it. She consoled herself, *maybe the weaver darned it so well that I can't detect the repair.* She ran her fingers along the base of the platform that the woven Amman was seated on. She discovered this space was bare.

Allarmelu distinctly remembered that the weaver of her ancestors' sari had embroidered his name in cenTamil: *S. Veerappan.* She remembered the brightness of the yellow silk thread for the name. Beside his name had run another word that rippled like a string of jasmine all along the border. The sari on her lap was an imposter!

Where is my mother's sari? The question became a mantra that repeated itself throughout the next few hours, even while she was telling Cook to grind the poppy seeds and coconut smoother than before for the noolkol korma, so it would slip down easily for her father, and supervising the picking of the red stones out of the gajjarasi rice.

The Imposter

Madras, April 1915

All her life Allarmelu got everything she wanted. It took a while for things to materialize by her standards of immediacy, but she got it all the same. Chellamma had taken care not to give in to her sulking. Kanna was held as a paragon of patience and was duly rewarded. While Allarmelu saw the virtue of patience, a quality she was unfamiliar with, she knew that the sari was not going to drop into her lap if she sat patiently. She decided that the need of the moment was rage. She was furious that anyone could insult her family's honour by replacing the original sari with an imposter. She could barely stop herself from twitching with rage.

In the past, when Allarmelu quarrelled with the women in the household, she would fly into a rage and bite her lip so hard, it bled. Rage after rage, Chellamma dabbed Allarmelu's lower lip with a soft muslin cloth dipped in turmeric, whispering, 'Amman, O Amman! you gave me this girl, please calm her down!'

Allarmelu's favoured goddess from the pantheon of Hindu deities was Amman, the guardian of neighbourhoods in cities and villages. A goddess with ten arms holding a sword, spear, alms bowl, sugarcane stalk,

sudarsana disc, rosary, book, scythe and a parrot perched
on her right shoulder. From the arms closest to her
body, Amman's left palm faced the worshipper assuring
protection, and the right palm pointed to her feet. It
was the path to surrendering the ego—that obstacle
to freedom. Allarmelu had never associated bowing at
Amman's feet as an act of 'surrender'. She translated it as
an initiation of *becoming* the force that is Amman. She felt
Shakti, the feminine force, the current that passed from
her mother to her, and she would not be denied the hunt
to restore the sari to its rightful heir. After all, Allarmelu
told herself, that sari is my birthright. It is the history of
all our mothers and their daughters.

Allarmelu felt the whole business of being bigger
than a 'big girl' was now laden with the responsibility of
assuring that the adult family members did not succumb
to death by gossip. It was commonplace rumour that
betrayals within families, in the name of family honour,
caused premature deaths. If that was the case, the first
casualty would be Jagan, her father. Then, Gowri and
Ruku, her aunts. Sadly, the cause of this series of tragic
premature deaths by gossip all led to the greatest obstacle
to living life with honesty, honour and harmony—her
father's very own brother Dharma. He was out and about
in the world without a clue about whom to trust or how
things really worked. He found it incomprehensible, she
realized, to consider the consequences of his actions on
the entire family. It was the direct result of his dandyism
and deluded aspirations of independence. She felt
protective towards him, as well as betrayed. She wanted
to shake him till his stupidity was dashed to the ground;
very much the way Nataraja danced on the Dwarf of

Ignorance in that bold Chola bronze that stood at the entrance to the *Surya Vilas* hallway.

She fortified herself with arguments against the wave of rising guilt. She wanted her mother's sari and she had the tenacity to seek it out. Should she upset her aunts' futures and hurt her father? How could she be denied what was hers, the sari that her mother had worn? She saw how much was invested in women keeping the family name for men, and the greatest betrayal was that Dharma was not aware of the 'imposter', or worse still, was he? She couldn't help feeling her aunts were justified in taunting him: 'Dharma is always in the reclining position...'

Patience was not the need of the hour. In any case, it was not a part of her arsenal as a course to action. She got herself into a state of frenzy: she was ready to avenge the injustice to her mother, to a temple sari, to women, to weaving, to Indian history itself. Even if she didn't have the words to express it, Allarmelu saw the sari as a tapestry of time weaving a hidden history of womens' genealogy. It was as significant to have a sari from your mother as it was to have a house of one's own. It was more than symbolic identity; it was economic independence.

She began to count on her fingers the number of days that had elapsed from the picnic in December 1909, when she was nine years old to when Pongal occurred. *Surya Vilas* was in mourning so there were no celebrations for Pongal. It was more than a month, so why did Chinnaina promise Amma and not keep his word?

Promises are broken when people become selfish because they do not get what they want when they want it, she decided. Even though she was alone, the voices in her head were howling the way the wind and the rain had during last November's monsoon. She cupped her ears. 'Enough!' she protested to herself.

The grave question staring at her, weighing heavier than all the silver and brass utensils in the kitchen was: *Does Naina know?* She knew neither Gowri nor Ruku would have had the guts to tell their elder brother that Chellamma had offered the sari to Dharma for repair. It was never spoken about, but well understood in the family, that Dharma was never serious about most matters. He was for all purposes 'BA-attempted-but-failed' and fit for nothing else but fine clothes and banter. But Chellamma had always included him in decisions about the family and its businesses. Allarmelu could still hear her mother's sorrow about the sari not returning to *Surya Vilas* before the Pongal festival.

Now that Allarmelu had 'attained puberty' she decided she too was a grown-up and would ask her Chinnaina directly about the missing sari, before she disclosed the fact to her father. But strangely, and for the first time, something made her hesitate. Was it because she was a woman now? She didn't know where Dharma lived. After Chellamma's death, he had disappeared under his wet, black umbrella for years. Later, she was aware from visiting relatives that he was back, and in circulation, but he never appeared at *Surya Vilas*. Her father had mentioned in passing that Dharma had entered the accounting side of the business and kept long hours at the office in Egmore. It was evident there would be no home visits. How could she possibly go and find him without everybody knowing about it? She could almost see the matchmakers hunched with relish, gossiping: *Allarmellu went to seek her Chinaina! What will any four people say?*

Which prospective bridegroom will accept that! She blurted out: 'Pah! Curling tongues like pariah dogs' tails will wag!'

Later that afternoon, one of Allarmelu's English governesses who, like her predecessors, had unsuccessfully completed her term at *Surya Vilas*, came to visit her aunts. Allarmelu heard her singing hymns to accompaniment on the piano. This was inevitably followed by elocution tuition with Gowri and Ruku. It concluded every fortnight with donations for the lace-making widows in the nearby convent at Vepery.

Allarmelu remained in the women's quarters upstairs till she heard the coach on the driveway. It had been sent to collect the 'Gowner Amma', as the governess was called. Allarmelu was never sure whether this was a reference to the English woman's gown, or the fact that she was a 'governor' because she was European and the 'v' was pronounced as an 'ow' by Tamil and Telugu speakers at *Surya Vilas*. That evening, Gowri and Ruku accompanied the 'Gowner' on a trip to Elliot's Beach to take the sea air.

Allarmelu heard the coach drive away, and smelt the vapour from the watered soil in the terracotta pots rising in the heat. The flowers from the coral wood tree fell to the percussion of their rattling pods and spat red streaks on the ground. How she missed Kanna, who gathered the parijata flowers by this time for the evening prayers.

Strands of jasmine wrapped in a dripping banana leaf, to keep their fragrance, were delivered by Joseph Perumal. Allarmelu started lighting the oil lamps in the family shrine room to take down to her father's study. Preparing the cotton wicks and dousing them with the homemade

ghee took a while. The grandfather clock struck
5:30 p.m. There were twenty-two lamps and each one
had five wicks. Allarmelu carefully replaced each lamp
on the altar after tapering the cotton wicks, and found
herself growing calm. But the strains of William Blake's
poem that the Governess had read out to Gowri and
Ruku earlier kept rising in her ears. 'Dark satanic mills.'
That stuck. It was Buckingham and Coromandel Mills!
The bag that carried her mother's wedding sari. She could
hear herself groan with impatience at one stubborn wick
in the lamp that was hissing, as it had got wet from a
fallen jasmine. The cyclone of questions started whirling
through her tangled thoughts again—about her Dharma
Chinaina and where the sari could have gone.

It was cow-dust hour, and from the window of the
shrine room she saw a new cartload of Pongam branches.
These were stacked beside the cow shed for fodder. In a
typical Madras way, the evening would suddenly turn to
night. She heard her father practicing the scales on his
fiteel. She was so preoccupied she hadn't heard him go
past the creaking stair. She thought she would swiftly
descend the stairs on tiptoe so her anklets wouldn't make
too much sound and light the oil lamp in front of the
Tanjavur Krishna in his study. She quickly circled the
lamp around the Vishnu and Lakshmi images, uttered a
short prayer that ended on 'courage, strength to banish all
delusion'. She knelt, and then scurried down the steps.

That's when she saw the front door opening quietly.
It was Dharma. He looked distraught. His jubba was
unbuttoned, his eyes were red, streaming with tears.
Unshaven and uncombed, she thought he looked like a
poet bereft of his muse. With all his study of Literature,

if only he could reflect the way Purandarasa did, about his past indulgences, replacing gold rings for tanboora strings and sing songs to wake us up from delusions!

Dharma seemed oblivious to her presence on the landing. She stood still on the staircase, partly cloaked in shadow. To her left was Jagan's library where Dharma was heading in a somnambulistic daze. The lamps had been lit and the light streamed onto the floor through the half-open doorway. The soft purple haze of the samrani frankincense trailed into the hallway, driving clusters of mosquitoes singing out of the room.

'Dharma?' Allarmelu heard her father call out. Dharma had barely stood in the doorway when Jagan gave instructions in Telugu. 'Do you see that leather case on my desk? Open it. Bring that book that's in it. Sit in that chair opposite me under the light. Start reading it to me… *I* know why that sari is important. But *you* need to understand.'

Allarmelu's stomach lurched. *Naina knows!* She was so shocked that he was aware that Chellamma gave the sari to Dharma, she nearly gasped out loud. She decided to stand, watch and hear what was to unfold.

'Anna,' Dharma was trying to hold back his tears, 'why do you say it like that? Spare me this while I am still remembering the goodness of Chellamma-anni.'

'Grieving for the dead is one thing and remembering them is another. The difference is that I am trying to awaken and save what is left of you in her memory. That was *my* Chellamma's, and your anni's greatest cry. *When will our Dharmipinnadu grow up? He has everything and yet he squanders life so…* she would tell me. She cared for you as if you were a son. Now she's gone, I'm trying to keep that promise.'

'Why do you all treat me like a child!'

'Because you go through life as if everything comes from the clouds! All this, the chair you sit on, the roof over our heads was possible after so many generations of hard work. You are spilling money through your fingers...' Jagan's tone remained calm. 'Ok, you want to be a man. An adult. Then face the fact of our turbulent history!'

Dharma stood at the table with his hands on the brown case. He lifted the lid and took out a frayed but well-bound brown leather book. He held it in his hands and said without agitation to his older brother, 'all I want is to be treated as a man. All I want is independence, to think, to act'.

'Then first you need to learn what it means to serve. Our way is to serve as a part of the whole. Every family member offers something to the larger family; if not with money or houses, then with love and respect for the history of a people, and what they hold so dear. Bring that book here. Come, sit by the light, and read every word aloud to me as you did in the days you were reading English Literature.'

Jagan said it with such tenderness that Dharma's nose too was streaming. He opened the book, took out his crumpled monogrammed kerchief, wiped his eyes and blew his nose, and then started reading. Allarmelu, fixed to the spot, moved without a sound into the study where she heard her Uncle's resonant voice reading the history of her mother's sari.

Book Two

Imminent Discovery

It was never my intention to write or keep a diary. My life as a governess was as steady as it was uneventful, and did not merit a record of daily occurrences. That is, until I met Jason Melville. He taught me to regard myself as a person independent of my service to the House of Grace. He drew attention to my difference, which gave me a sense of esteem, and commended my adaptation to the environment that was so alien to my origin. For good or for ill, it is due to this encouragement I begin this story of myself. I have learned much by reading and observing the example others have lived by. My life may not teach much, but I write it to remind myself of my own history.

Mr Whippett was visiting for tea. I had been in his charge all the way from India, while being brought to Lord and Lady Grace's home in England. My position as Governess there came with a great many letters of recommendation from the convent in Calcutta, where I had been placed under care. Mr Whippett, who was associated with all sorts endeavouring to do good to humanity, saw me there. He decided that once my English was as good spoken as it was written, then the time would be right 'in the year of Our Lord 1866 to arrive on the shores of civilization where young orphaned women could make a living through learning and serving'.

It was clear I was not going to be made a nun. I did not possess the requisite loyalty to a singular vision of God. While boarding at the convent, each time we girls, mostly orphans, sat in St Mary's chapel, I looked at Jesus's mother, and thought of Amman and prayed that she would look after all of humanity the way Jesus's mother cared over him. Soon, Mother Mary and Amman became one for me and I felt happy. Every time we were told to repeat the rosary, I would say the Hail Mary out loud and continue to repeat in my mind 'o mariamman, o karimariamman, o ponniamman, o gangamman...' That was fine. I had two worlds that kept me safe, and no one got hurt. The problem was when I fell ill and had very high fever. I was delirious and kept repeating 'Amman o Amman', while clutching my rosary. This was overheard and reported. My belongings were searched and the small black stone statue of Amman that the Kurathai woman had given me was 'confiscated and exorcized. I was made to repent for being ungrateful to the kindness and compassion shown to me by the Church and convent, as I had evidently harboured faith in idol worship, secretly. I learned so many words at that time, and 'sin' was one of them.

Without being taught, I learned that actually these were words that constructed a labyrinth of hatred born of fear, for things that people were not willing to understand. I didn't have language then to explain. Would they have listened? But I will never forget their kindness. I digress.

I must return to the evening Mr Whippett came to visit. As his letter indicated, he wanted to enquire how his

'Indian Charge, now the new Governess of your esteemed Lord and Lady Grace, was conducting herself and her responsibilities in relation to the Christian education of the children'.

Lord and Lady Grace good-humouredly read the letter out to me at least a month before his arrival. I had now been two years in their service and had found the composure necessary to discharge my duties, as well as company in Lady Grace, interest in the children's progress, and hope in Lord Grace's Library, which he allowed me to use from time to time when it was appropriate to pursue my own education.

Earlier that afternoon I was rung for and proceeded to the drawing room in my slate-grey dress and starched white collar, parted with the mother-of-pearl brooch. 'Dear C, we will have to call you by your Christian name when Mr Whippet is with us'. Lady Grace looked at me with that twinkle in her eye. Happiness always fluttered in the rooms that she inhabited.

'Yes, Ma'am', I said, as we both smiled the way women do when men are not in the room. All social barriers of titles and hierarchies were down, but we continued the choreography of Mistress and servant in our terms of address to each other.

Lord Grace ambled into the drawing room cradling his volume of *Sartor Resartus* in his large right hand, with Finch, the bloodhound, by his side. The hound and Lord Grace looked like a portrait in grey; his grey trousers and coat, grey hair softly framing his face with his grey sideburns. When he looked up from his book, his dark brows leapt and his grey eyes danced at the sight of his wife.

'And what great glimmers of wisdom is Carlyle to give us this afternoon my Lord, your heavenly grace?' asked Lady Grace. Husband and wife laughed companionably at her mock deference. I shifted as if to excuse myself out of their private company.

'No, C, do stay. It will soon be time. I don't want to exert myself to ring for you again. Mr Whippett arrives at four. Before then, I'd like his Lordship to taste this.'

She held out the gilded plate, embossed with the Grace coat-of-arms—a shield and quill, in grey lined with red and gold. At the moment it was hidden by a steaming hot idli and a dollop of chutney.

He tasted it. 'Mm! Superlative! What is it?'

'An Idlee! Indian rice dumplings, darling. C was so kind to make them herself. Can you imagine the chaos it caused for Mrs T in the kitchen? What with all the maids sneezing because of the spices! Would you believe it!' They both laughed generously and I joined in. I was delighted they had enjoyed the small idlis, steamed and served with the tomato chutney to which I had added only cumin and just one dried red chilli.

There was still a half an hour to go for the arrival that I neither dreaded nor welcomed. I had schooled myself over the years to expect an unforeseen change in my circumstances at any moment, without notice. I couldn't have wished for a better situation than the one I was in now, and a dismissal caused by any stray occurrence would wound me most, as it would betray the trust that Lady Grace in particular, and Lord Grace and the children had placed in me. For the first time in a long while, I felt some peace with my surroundings, and a sense of inner strength.

Outside, along the flint wall, a carriage followed by a cart was winding along the driveway. I loved to watch how, at first, you would only see the image of something approaching soundlessly, then as it drew closer; you could hear the grinding of the wheels on the stone till it halted in the porch—the way the sense of something occurs only after sighting it.

Finch loped out of the door to investigate and bayed so loudly that the three of us laughed, acknowledging Lady Grace's caption for the sound he made: 'The Lament for Beowulf'. Lord Grace deftly dipped his fingers into the China bowls of water that I had instructed be kept handy while the idli was being served. He wiped his lips with the napkin and stuffed it into his coat, so as not to leave any evidence on the table of having eaten before a guest's arrival. Lady Grace arranged herself on the Queen Anne chair so her head rested on the left wing, and they both regained their composure to receive 'god's own servant', Mr Whippett.

Mr Whippett was a short man with no neck and his oversized collars looked like something between a ruff and a wreath. His bald head gleamed more than I had remembered. I had last seen him when I was appointed to the Graces' home. He had not lost his vanity in believing that he had hair enough to drag across his head from one side to the other, which sadly made him look like a man sitting uncomfortably between two banks of time— uncouth youth and unseemly age.

I had learned from an early age never to show what I really thought or felt, as I was always a stranger, even to people I was familiar with. Lady Grace was consciously not catching her husband's eye as Mr Whippett made his entrance. He stood a few feet into the drawing room, framed by the oak doorway, and did a salutation where he had his right hand on his heart and bowed low, remaining thus for almost a minute. We all saw his head turn red as a summer peach when he raised himself from that deferential position. It was a salutation I had seen in paintings where Royalty knighted men. It certainly caused much embarrassment to the liberalism of the Grace home.

I daresay I was touched by Mr Whippett's salutation, as it combined the Indian gesture of humility with an English feudal greeting. This was the connection that Lord Grace and Mr Whippett shared: Englishmen with interests in India. One was a man of inheritance and wealth connected with trade; the other was a man trading a mission.

'Greetings!' Mr Whippett's voice rang as if he were in a congregation, as he straightened himself and surveyed the room, with its carpets, paintings, drapes, and chandeliers, before he rested his gaze of appreciation on Lady Grace. Lord Grace approached to shake his hand.

'Miss Christina, how well you look! And that is all thanks to the beneficence of Lord and Lady Grace!' Mr Whippet's etiquette was immaculate and studied, with occasional strokes of genuine human kindness. My life had been transformed by his kindness that had transported me from one world to another—India to England. He ended each pronouncement with a little grunt that was meant to be a laugh of social ease, but at times it had the contrary effect of ingratiating social awkwardness.

I curtsied, 'As do you, Sir.'

After a few pleasantries were exchanged about the weather and how there was a change of seasons unlike what we knew before, Mr Whippett cleared his throat. We sat enthralled, listening to his extraordinary account of a very ordinary journey across the flatness of Norfolk. We could have clapped at the end, but Lady Grace pre-empted our mischievous intent and rang for tea.

'And the children, Master Stephen and Miss Isobel? How are they progressing in their instruction from Miss Christina?' Mr Whippett was genuinely interested in their education, which included the geography of India and its plant life.

'Very well indeed. In fact C…er…Miss Christina has actually impressed on them the qualities of heat, and humidity in the geography lesson. Now that's exceptional teaching wouldn't you say?' said Lord Grace.

'Indeed! Then it must be observed that the intelligence of Master Stephen at ten years of age is exceptional as well? I would say the Navy for him!' Mr Whippett had the incurable habit of finding a lifetime profession for whomsoever passed his way.

Lady Gray had suggested a recital by the children for the occasion. I had supervised long hours of rehearsal and by this time they were ready to burst with their accomplishments for Mr Whippett's enlightenment of my proficiency in teaching and the children's ability in learning. Lady Grace nodded at me to bring the children in. I excused myself and as Master Stephen and Miss Isobel were rehearsing in the adjacent room, we swiftly returned to the drawing room. Tea had been poured. The aroma of scones, marmalade cake and the steaming idlis filled the corner of the drawing room where everyone was seated.

Master Stephen and Miss Isobel were looking forward to their moment of performance and I couldn't help congratulating myself as I watched their deportment. Miss Isobel suddenly saw the marmalade cake and her eyes widened. Her one great weakness was cake. However, being as thin as a reed gave her an advantage over most human beings in being able to consume vast quantities of it. I was more concerned by her being distracted by it, which would throw her concentration off, rather than any imminent consequence to her health. She decided to hasten proceedings in the hope of securing it as a reward. She struck the bow on her violin. It screamed. And she said, 'We *will* begin.'

Mr Whippett jumped. He spluttered the tea he was sipping and recovered instantly by rearranging himself in the chair to face the next generation of the family of the House of Grace.

Miss Isobel's recital of *Twinkle Twinkle Little Star* on the violin was applauded. Thankfully, she looked at me for approval, with one foot set on her marks to go and eat the marmalade cake. My stare must have stung the child so that she stood limp in that spot. Master Stephen had his turn at elocution with a brief passage from memory from *Epicedium On the Death of Lord Nelson*.

While notes of triumph swell the gale,
Why sits BRITANNIA sad and pale
In the hour of victory?
She mourns her gallant Hero dead,
She weeps that matchless NELSON bled,
And pensive bows her laurel'd head,
In the hour of victory!

Chief of the lion's dauntless soul,
From Egypt's shore to Norway's pole,
'Twas thine to bid my thunders roll,
In the hour of victory!
Teach thou the valiant, good and great,
Thy high exploits to emulate,
And fearless smile like thee on fate,
In the hour of victory!'

Master Stephen's elocution enthralled Mr Whippett, who tapped the metre of the poem on his knee. 'Bravo! Encore!' said the adults. It was a transformation. I could see how overwhelmed Lady Grace was at Master Stephen's rendition; she had feared her son's stammer would impair his life when I had first joined service. Master Stephen was so relieved he looked pale. I swiftly served him a large slice of Mrs T's marmalade cake. He looked at me with such gratitude that my eyes smarted with tears. I knew it wasn't for the marmalade cake; it was for the hours spent over the course of a year coaxing him to read poems out loud. His face would go eggshell-pale and speckled at what seemed a challenge. Then, engaging him in the tapping of the metre, I'd watch his grey eyes work out the puzzle between letters and rhythmic patterns and the meaning locked behind the words. It was the way I had learned English. 'Nandri', he whispered, looking up at me as I served him the cake. The Tamil word for 'thank you' that I had taught him when we were looking at words from various languages that had similar meanings across all cultures.

The atmosphere in the room heightened, melded with relief, congratulatory pride and merriment, as even

Finch did a turn by baying on cue when the children took a bow. While Mr Whippett was demolishing a second scone, both Lord and Lady Grace caught my eye, and their smiles made my heart swell, knowing I had earned my place.

Finch flapped his ears and jowls. The sky was growing darker with looming thunderclouds and the wind had started a howl. In spite of Mr Whippett's early arrival, and the tea finishing early, I could see the children were exhausted from their recital, the excitement that preceded it, the preparation and the acclaim with which it was received. I led them out to the Nursery with the Graces' permission. They requested me to return to their company in the drawing room.

It must have taken a half hour to settle the children and when I returned to the drawing room all the chandeliers were lit. It seemed as if what had passed before was a dream.

Mr Whippett and Lord Grace were standing with their backs to the entrance of the drawing room, and the two porters who had driven the cart accompanying the carriage, had just set down a very heavy ebony settee. It had been placed by the western wall of the drawing room, just under the two prized paintings by Turner, work he had completed a few years before he died—a wedding gift to the Graces. Both were my favourite works in the house, of Hero and Leander, and of Undine the mermaid giving the ring to a fisherman from Naples. So undoubtedly, the settee belonged to a place of special sentiment. In spite of the wind and autumnal chill outdoors, Lady Grace was using her lace hand-fan to keep cool, with yet another chapter of excitement that evening.

The jute-sack wrapping around the settee was ripped open to reveal flaming orange silk against the ebony. My heart skipped a beat.

'The carving is intact! Absolute craftsmanship! Splendid, quite splendid,' said Lord Grace as he invited Lady Grace to trace the carving with her fingers.

'A Coromandel settee! All the way from Madras, Christina. You must tell us what the carvings are all about in the morning light. This is a wonderful surprise!' said Lady Grace as she flicked shut her fan.

Lord Grace was pleased and turning to Mr Whippett said, 'that was jolly decent of you to have them shipped across well before I expected them! I think that calls for a whisky, don't you?' It was an offer that Mr Whippett could not decline, and his eyes sparkled with fulfilment at the recognition from the Graces of his immaculate planning and execution.

I sat on the chaise longue, my back upright, facing the settee with its flaming orange seat cover woven in silk. I realized again that one sees an image, or object, and only after a while makes sense of it. I was for that moment sitting 'blind'. Sitting, admiring the settee, the Coromandel settee. When it was unwrapped, it smelt of the air of a place, bringing a memory from a time I had forced myself to forget.

'I'm impressed that you should have got these safely here, Mr Whippett' said Lord Grace, while sipping his whisky.

'Yes, it was unfortunate that so much was lost—lives and property. I rest happily in the belief some were saved by our Mission', Mr Whippett said, suddenly sounding pensive.

'So what brought it all on? And, to such exorbitant proportions in the cost of human lives? Surely all we mean to do there is good?' said Lady Grace, genuinely alarmed in case the truth may be to the contrary.

'So many views get expressed. But finally we have to hold on to those who protect the commonwealth of Her Majesty's government…' said Mr Whippet.

'But surely', Lord Grace interrupted. 'That's the point of *Sartor Resartus*, isn't it? *The Tailor Retailored*.' We all looked blankly at him as none of us had read the book he had brought in with him. He read our expressions and proceeded without impatience: 'We are introduced to Diogenes Teufelsdröckh, a German philosopher of clothes, who is in fact a creation of Carlyle's. Of course, it's purely to comment on the way the British Public is swept by a commercial wave of utility. We are re-tailoring justice and making a virtue of greed!'

'But no one is getting to the point. What *is* it all about?' Lady Grace asked the question with a sense of enquiry bordering on the imminent discovery of an unpalatable truth.

'Well that's why it's called a "Mutiny", dear! The Indians were protesting against the command of the British Garrison by not obeying orders to use animal fat on the bullets. I daresay that was unreasonable, getting hindoos to handle cow fat, and moslems pig fat to grease the cartridges…' said Lord Grace.

'Well on one side, it was a holy animal, the cow, and on the other side, pork is the work of the devil…' interjected Mr Whippett when he found a chance, in Lord Grace's full flow. 'But that is one side to the news. The other, of course, is that it is a rebellion against Her Majesty's government, as they laid siege on Delhi and decided to proclaim their King as the Emperor of Hind. How *can* that be possible?'

'I just don't understand who's at war anymore across India. There are the Afghans, and us, and Indian princedoms…so who are the Indian soldiers fighting for, or against?' asked Lady Grace.

'Dangerous questions darling. Yes, I can only surmise our first intention was to trade. Now that business is good, and with the East India Company financing an Army, it's taking on another colour.' Lord Grace pursed his lips in resignation at the flow of events and suddenly looked morose.

'I think it would be truthful to say the whole incident of '57 and how it fanned India with a fire of discontent, was a misunderstanding.'

'A misunderstanding?!'

I had no idea who had said it or when I had got up from my seat or excused myself—I must have, otherwise Lady Grace would certainly have called me. I was going to swoon from the damp cold working its way up my back, leaving it painfully tight. I was feeling sick. My head was hot and thumping, and when I came out of the drawing room, all I remember was the click of the doorknob pressing the lock into the matching door. I was shivering and perspiring at the same time. I wanted to run, undoing my hair, the stays from my dress, collar, the brooch, fling my shoes the way Miss Isobel did when she was upset, but I made it up the steep stairs to my room at the top—sick of my ability to remain sane. I wanted to scream.

I went as swiftly as I could over the forty-eight steep

steps. When I unlocked my room, I scrambled to the small cabinet beside my bed near the door, and grabbed the flask that stood there. I clutched it for comfort as I had been taught to do with the Hail Mary rosary. Thankfully the fire had not died down, so I stoked it between swigs of the brandy we were allowed solely for medicinal purposes. Then I stood with my back to the fireplace. The feeling of warmth from the flames turning to heat along the sides of my spine made my back relax, and my shoulders and fingers literally bloom, the way plantains do. I could feel, and see, and think again.

I looked out of the window. The view I had from my room so high up overlooking the rear garden was as exquisite as it was treacherous. The grey clouds had lifted, leaving a kingfisher-blue sky streaked with crimson and gold where the sun was setting. The west wind was buffeting horse chestnut trees, the way I had seen boys from the orphanage shake young trees of their leaves. It always started with a sense of play as the boys would climb the branches and swing on them, sometimes snapping twigs and shaking dry leaves down. Then I would watch play turn to fury as if they were shaking Fate itself off from the leaves of the book that had determined their unfortunate destinies. Now, outside the window, the leaves were spinning like tops. The light from the fading sky caught them whirling down, and they blazed like copper, brass, gold. All the leaves were pulled to land in mounds on the sodden black earth. I thought of goddess Amman as Kali, in her form of the blackness of Time. All these floating leaves, like soulless bodies, would turn to coal, in time, just like the blazing embers that were keeping me warm now.

The stars blinked as night bled indigo into what was the day. It was the transition from pain to comfort, from damp cold to dry heat that made me stop, and take a breath and reflect. What was it that had happened earlier in the evening that had made me freeze?

My mind kept shuffling for images to articulate what I felt. Master Stephen owned a fossil given him by a collector. I couldn't help thinking of it now. Fish frozen over time, in rocks that were now surrounded by land and nowhere near the sea. My sense of time and place had frozen that way. What was the story about these fish-rocks? How did their bones become part of a landscape so full of vegetation? Had the seas receded? Were the fish-rocks a measure of land underwater? These landmasses had emerged and were continents now. What was my story? At least the fish-rock had stayed in one place and had unravelled a story about time on earth. I had been churned in the stormy teacup of History's currents from one continent to another. And then, I let out a howl.

It all came back, vividly.

Chandrika

Coromandel Coast, c.1848

I was told my birth was on mid year's night, when the moon was full and Amman at her temple was offered thread, cloth, food, music and dance, and She held her weavers in trance.

In the village of my birth there were huts thatched with palmyra fronds where the dyers of yarn lived, and some weavers had small houses where the looms were kept. Even if I don't remember the details of its alleys, wells, or names, the memory of the husk of the paddy rising in a soft haze, mixed with the dust from drying red chillies that burned in your breath, visits me in my sleep, along with images of low doorways and sun-splattered inner courtyards. But most of all, I remember with the rhythm of my heartbeat, the click-click clacking of the loom.

My father was a weaver and our house had a tiled roof. Beyond the inner courtyard stood his loom. Its legs were the height of a two-year-old child, standing. The yarns along the warp and across the weft of loom were always two different colours that melded where the cloth had been woven. There was cloth woven for Amman at the temple. There was cloth woven to cover utensils for rituals. There were saris woven for weddings. Silk and gold.

It was not until I was nine years old that I was taught how to learn what a sari speaks. Its stick figures—girls were marked with strands of long hair; men had hair knotted into a bun on the nape of the neck; goatherds had another stick, following a goat—were finely woven in contrasting colours. Figures with stick legs and arms but vibrant with the joy of dance. A ball was a rudraksh bead, bigger than the stick chasing it. A peacock's unfurled tail meant a wedding, or dated it as woven in the monsoon. A tiger's head—the season of drought or danger. Elephants in masth—the mating season.

One sari, the only one given to me in my name is the story I tell myself; a story about my beginnings.

In the season of Aadi, it was the first cloudless night that month and the full moon asserted itself in the sky once the celebrations had quietened. Fatima crept out from one of the low-lying huts after the last of the embers from the cooking fire died out. She dragged her weight with its protruding belly past a symphony of snoring men, waving aside clouds of mosquitoes. She staggered up to the mango grove, away from the circle of palm-thatched huts. She edged her way, ducking and diving between low boughs and through fingers of moonlight. There was a clearing. The moon dazzled her with its paving of light.

Fatima kept muttering 'Further, deeper, Amma, Devi'. The guardian goddess of the forest was summoned, and Fatima felt a new surge of energy carry her across the clearing into the jungle.

A frog was croaking. It couldn't be for more rain. Every little ditch had become a pond serenaded by a halo of mosquitoes. The lilac flowers of the water hyacinth glowed. As she entered the jungle where the moonlight could not seep through, fireflies were lighting the dark.

The only response to Fatima's feet brushing past leaves and snipping twigs was an old white owl's hooting. The frog continued its lament, so familiar to villagers, when transfixed by the cobra's spread hood and bejewelled neck.

The smell of soggy wood and soaked dead foliage wrapped itself around Fatima like an anxious, unwanted relative. The occasional drift of the nocturnal jasmine's perfume revived her from the isolation of her mission. The pain in her body was going to explode. She found an even spot where the moon shone through, then spread the plantain leaf she had been carrying from her hut. She squatted on it. In her right hand she clutched a crescent-shaped sickle. Fatima took comfort in the frog song and punctuated its silences with 'Amma, Devi, kapathu Thali'. With every heaving breath, she pushed harder, and the frog song grew quieter. It stopped. The cobra must have struck and swallowed the frog into its sleek blackness.

Silence. Fatima screamed and the wet creature she had in her belly sluiced through her large warm blackness into a tiny sphere of light on the plantain leaf. Ecstatic, hysterical, crying, laughing, Fatima's incantations to 'Amma, Devi, Thali' changed from pleading to praise. She sought the goddess's protection over and over again, 'kapathu Ma, kapathu'.

The placenta was delivered. Trembling, she smoothed the child's body, anointed with her mucous and blood. Then, gripping the sickle, she severed the umbilical cord. With all the breath in her body she cried out 'AMMA!'

It rent the air, and shook the leaves on the branches. Even the spot of moonlight quivered as the owl fluttered across the trees to another perch. The earth sighed as Fatima slumped with joy.

Karpu, the black pariah dog with his white-tipped ringtail and muzzle, had a keen scent for births, deaths, strangers, friends and spies. His vocal cords adapted to the celebratory or commiserating note appropriate to each occasion. He had raised a soft growl when he saw Fatima leaving the hut. When he heard an owl flutter, he yowled, his head high up to the sky. Then he whimpered, panted and began barking. Veerappan, his master, couldn't sleep. With the respite from rain over the last two days, the water level had receded. Rats and bandicoots were scampering over sleeping children and attacking the household terracotta pots stored with grain.

From that distance between the jungle and the huts, Veerappan heard Fatima's muffled cry of 'AMMA'. It wasn't uncommon for villagers going to relieve themselves at night to encounter jackals and hyenas, and sometimes there were tigers. As the unofficial caretaker of the village, he raised the alarm. The men stumbled out of their sleep and gathered up thick bamboo sticks. Some carried their sickles. The fear of harm descending on a child-bearing woman such as Fatima, and the belief that a curse would follow on the village, drove the men in herds into the jungle.

Karpu's scent was the only lead for the search party. Once they entered the jungle, the cicadas engulfed them in a deafening roar. The night jasmine unfurled its heady fragrance and the older men shuddered, as they knew that snakes must be close by. How carefully could they tread on slithering leaves? Every wet twig under their bare feet began to feel like a moving floor of snakes.

Karpu whimpered and dashed ahead, following the trail of human scent. Soon the smell of blood was rising like fish and Veerappan held the others back. The smooth spot of moonlight had shifted and was now dappled by shadows of leaves. Veerappan stepped cautiously into the clearing; the clanging in his temples drowning the sound of crickets.

The body of Fatima lay with her legs forming a triangle cradling the newborn that glistened with the mucous encasing it. Veerappan's heart stopped. Then a rush of blood made it start again, loudly. Kneeling, with a blade of moonlight glinting on the shiny threads of his shoulder cloth, he picked up the screaming infant and held it close to his heartbeat. Then freeing his right arm, he ripped the amulet around his neck, spat out its cap and poured the honey held in it into the infant's mouth.

Some distance away the others watched. Karpu kept licking Fatima's legs, then, face. Her half-open palm was holding a swatch of moonlight.

'Well,' said Ellam looking at Fatima's bare legs, 'that was the tastiest dish our grandmothers served up in a long time!'

Kunni sucked long and hard on his glowering beedi. As he exhaled, the white wisps of tobacco smoke hung in the air like clouds. 'Dai! The same tongue that is titillated by taste now will be licking flames of fire on that pyre!'

'Enough! Has the rain washed off all memory of who lived and what they did for us?' Kumaran was at the back of the group. Pali was leaning his elbow on Ellam's shoulder and couldn't resist retorting. 'Ayiyiyo! There are enough years ahead for old age and epic talk. We were only admiring what was living.' The sniggering scattered unevenly and hushed as Kumaran advanced. His eyes burned and glistened like a snake. Pali shifted his weight from one bandy leg to the other awkwardly. He made a nervous attempt to spit out his phlegm, but decided it was safer to swallow it. Kumaran's contempt for Ellam and Pali's disregard of the dead quivered in his voice as he spoke:

'Dai! Have you no shame? You are nothing better than jackals.

Jackals are known to smile with buffalo
Warning him of lion's leap.
Jackals also smile with lion, disclosing buffalo's well-guarded retreat.
After the kill, lion takes his share;
Jackal is left with buffalo's testicles to eat!'

There was a pause. 'What does he think he's doing?' Murugan the elder whispered hoarsely, and everyone's attention was directed to Veerappan. All the men looked over Kumaran's shoulder as Veerappan bent down to raise Fatima's body. He touched his head three times to the earth near Fatima's feet, then raised the bundled infant to his head and held it up to the moon.

The villagers crept forward. They could see tears streaming down his cheeks. With a choked voice he solemnly uttered, 'Chandrika'. The others realized a girl had been born to the village. From that moment, they accepted Veerappan's decision to name me after the moon's ray that led them to me.

Seeraivakkam's Gift

In this village of Seeraivakkam, Amman the goddess is worshipped as a feminine force. She is Shiva's consort and a warrior. She is the essence of Being and is loved as the divine mother. For everyone at Seeraivakkam, Amman is a presence that protects the abandoned, the lover with an earnest heart. She cannot be restrained by borders of any kind and rewards friends and enemies alike.

It was so even for Fatima, who was among the few Muslims brought to Seeraivakkam as a bride. She was widowed within weeks of the first year of marriage. She stayed on because she, too, believed Amman would take care of her.

Seeraivakkam was not a village of farmers; it was a village of weavers, where Fatima's husband was born, apprenticed and worked. She had learned that the cycles of sowing, harvest and storage of paddy rice and seasonal vegetables took up one part of village life. But weaving was the craft, the trade, the passion. The art of the weaver was supreme, held above the rungs of Hindu caste. Every villager believed that humans are the thread, their religion the dye, the loom life itself and weaving the night and day of peoples' life stories.

Throughout the year, bullock-cart tracks were kept clear to other villages for trading woven cotton cloth that ranged from pandal marquees and mattress coverings to saris. There was high demand for cushions stuffed with cotton and mattress covers, to dress the Coromandel ebony settees that had been introduced into fashion in London. While Seeraivakkam's weavers made the cloth, in the neighbouring village of carpenters, looms and ebony settees were built. Together, these were transported on bullock carts to wait in warehouses in Fort St George in Madras before being shipped by Lloyds Shipping of the East India Company to London's Leadenhall Street.

The silkworms bred at the edge of the jungle gave Seeraivakkam its prestige in weaving yards of silk for ceremonies—and for the dresses and trousseaus of the Memsahibs who stepped off the ships at Fort St George, to wear during the string of balls in honour of visiting Viceroys, Governor Generals of India, the military and officials of the Company.

The zamindar landlords worshipped the soil of Seeraivakkam, where the trees for their wood grow to make the looms. From the looms, the yarn spins out stories. Stories telling, reciting, performing, the legend of Amman as warrior, protector, as Other, as lover, matriarch, and as the guardian of the arts. It is how the rituals across the festivals of the year are kept alive. From stories that that were told, motifs and symbols were created for weaving, and the weavers embedded these into their saris. These woven stories are the silent repository of generations of villagers, who lived, loved, fought, worshipped, and encountered the Shakti that is the life and feminine force of Amman.

The plants of the soil are sacred, as they heal the weavers when they are stung, bitten, or poisoned.

Weavers and dyers search for weeds and vegetables that give rich colours; the plants bleed colours into the yards of handspun thread, which is then woven into fabric. Livestock is reared and groomed for processional festivals in honour of Amman's dominant mood at the change of the seasons. Cows, in particular, are special: apart from giving milk for daily use, some of them are fed on mango leaves, for their urine, which seals the dye. It gives richness to the yellow clothing of the gods on temple wall hangings depicting the epics in a local landscape.

At the edge of the jungle, facing east, was a banyan tree whose hundreds of aerial roots formed an extended family of younger trees. Midway up the main trunk, a triangular niche was carved out, ornamented with a border of vermillion and three stripes of turmeric along its base and angles. Every morning, the earth was swept and a clay lamp with cotton wick doused in gingelly oil was lit by one of twelve women. Amman was propitiated at the snake holes underneath, where tiny clay cups were filled with milk and eggs, placed on Tuesdays. Great-grandmothers had passed the ritual of lighting lamps at sunrise and sunset to successive generations of daughters; to relay the light between the passage of night into day, and day into night.

That one year, the monsoon had flooded the paddy fields. Some of the cows, too, were swept away. The floodwater had raged like a domestic quarrel at night. In the past years, the level of the water often receded by morning. Women would wade through knee-deep water to get to the shrine and offer their worship. This year, the gingelly oil was adulterated. The cotton wick was damp, and the once-steady golden flame of the lamp sputtered

and hissed. Over the past few nights, the water level had
not receded. No one dared venture to light the lamp. Was
this an omen? Such thoughts hammered in the villagers'
sleep-torn minds.

When Fatima walked out of her hut, the villagers
knew it was impossible for a wild animal to maul her in
the high lustre of a full moon on a cloudless night, and
slept with that comforting thought. The moon paved
the clearing with its dazzling light as it had centuries
before, and would continue to do many centuries after,
like a woman smiling, imploring her lover to stay just a
few moments more, for the last time.

For a moment Seeraivakkam slept through the cries,
almost as if Fatima was the sacrifice to the elements.
Fatima knew the way Seeraivakkam thought: 'To be
awake and hear the cries and not do anything would
be considered sinful, but to be asleep while it happened
would be a blessing'.

That is the first memory I have. I remember my
mother's body sighing, as if from relief, and its imprint
remains with me. It was the sense that I was a blessing.

Ever since then, I remember her heartbeat as the
click-click-clacking of looms. I knew the man they
called Veerappan—the brave one—as my father. He sat
on the floor his legs straightened under the loom, as he
sang lullabys to the percussion of the loom. Chilli red,
turmeric yellow, paddy green, kingfisher blue, these were
the colours my eyes drank in as I lay held by one woman
or other who had milk in her breasts and nursed me with
her other children.

Pilgrims and Kuttu storytelling troupes visited
Seeraivakkam on festivals and stayed for three or four

days. The men wore brass bells around their ankles and carried brass or mud pots on their heads, filled with boiled milk, as they danced in a trance on a bed of burning embers to offer the gift of allegiance by performing stories about Amman. This happened every July, the Aadi masam.

During new year, around Pongal in February, cattle horns were anointed with stripes of turmeric and vermillion and capped with brass bells. The cows had their foreheads painted, with white and orange flower garlands around the folds of their necks. Everyone made pongal in front of their huts—rice and lentils cooked together in earthen pots over small fires fuelled by dried cow-dung cakes. You could hear the cheers of 'Pongal-o-pongal' running like a ribbon down all the interconnected alleys of Seeraivakkam. The rising smoke from the dung-cake fires would sting every child's eyes. But at least it kept the mosquitoes, geckos and rats away for a little while.

There is a festival dedicated to Amman who keeps the tracks clear so that Seeraivakkam is never flooded. Everyone joined in the processional prayer escorting the goods on bullock carts till it reached the Fort.

The years passed and I did not know how many. I knew by the colours how many threads were in Veerappan's loom. I don't remember how old I was, but I could understand what Veerappan meant when he said with tears in his eyes: 'I'm going to weave the ocean and its waves in this sari. Your name will run in the border with yellow—why, even gold thread if I can afford it—all along the nine yards: *chandrikachandrikachandrikachandrika*. It will be like those pomegranate pink sunsets followed by a ripple of moonlight on water.'

I had heard my name sung in lullabys as well as in temple dramas, and I knew what it meant. It rippled through my heart with a feeling I grew to call Love.

I remember a man, referred to as 'Secretary Sir Aiya', came to Seeraivakkam every month. He wore a turban, and had a big red dot in the centre of his forehead, his diamond earrings gleaming like miniature midday suns. He carried away jute sacks filled with rice. He would collect cloth, salt, and vegetables from all the villagers. We had grown up knowing the land we lived on was not our own, but we cared for it with our life. When he came, all the weavers from the village cleared a space under the mango tree in the centre of the encircling huts. He would bring out a big scroll and take an account of everyone, names of men, women and children—births, deaths, who was ill and checked the teeth of all of us children.

But one day he brought a man who had hair that shone like gold, with skin that was very pink, and golden eyebrows and lashes. He wore a red coat and was sweating profusely. He had shoes that were up to his knees and he was at least twenty yards above all of us, as he sat on his horse.

I was the last to run up. The villagers were in silent awe as they gazed up at the 'Military Sir'. The solitary clinking of my anklets caught his attention. He barked something, and Secretary Sir Aiya smiled greasily as he said, 'You must be assembled here before we arrive. We have much to do, and far to travel and can't be seen wasting our time waiting for you all at Seeraivakkam to wake up.'

'Is this clear?' shouted the Military Sir.

All of us at Seeraivakkam lurched a bit as if caught in a net the way fish are when pulled out of the water, realizing all too late they cannot escape.

Secretary Sir Aiya began administering the loading of vegetable baskets and sacks of rice into the bullock carts. All these goods were heaved in by seven weavers in a row—heave, pass, lunge and stack—and it went on and on, the repetition like the warp and the weft of the loom, but joyless. We children and the older men stood and watched as Amman's gifts to us of salt, silk, vegetables were being taken away. I wondered why would one man need so much? How many of our homes had families that ate only a handful of rice a day after working in the fields, grazing the goats, and fetching water from distant wells.

I stopped thinking as Secretary Sir Aiya flashed a smile. From under his waxed moustache, glinted a golden tooth. I had never seen anything like it before. His smile wasn't open like what I had seen among men in our village. It struck me that he was trying to show he was one of us when he wasn't. At the same time he showed he was above us, which he wasn't, as he was short and round. And at the very same time he wanted to show us he was with the Military Sir, even though he couldn't.

At his height on the horse, Military Sir certainly looked down on Secretary Sir Aiya and not for one moment treated him like a human. When Military Sir barked out his instructions it was to Secretary Sir Aiya; when he said 'Is that clear?' he looked at all of us villagers. Very confusing. After my first sight of him, Secretary Sir Aiya seemed to look like a jackal. The old stories told of how Jackal would make friends with Bull and Tiger. Then Jackal would lead Bull to be slaughtered by Tiger. From the remains of Bull, Jackal would have a sly pick at Tiger's meal and it was always to the sound of nervous laughter.

The next thing I remember was the Margayi masam or winter season. The lavender coloured flowers we called 'disember' were strung in the hair of all the women, except widows, in the village. Veerappan had finished the ocean-wave sari. He asked me to come and see it as it was spread out on his loom. The light that streamed in from the shuttered window caught the kingfisher-blue threads shot with purple. I nuzzled my face into the fabric. The smell of the loom and the scent of Veerappan's tobacco leaf lingered on it. I imagined I was riding on a peacock's tail out of the dark house, above the village and could see absolutely everything, and nothing in particular—it was a wonderful feeling. My cheek rested against the sari. Raw silk. Porous. It was second skin. Veerappan took my hand and made me run my finger over the golden threads that had *chandrikachandrikachandrikachandrikachandrika* running along the border. His fingers had joints the size of sambar onions and he worked and worked on the letters of my name. The twisting of the wiry gold thread to form the Tamil letters *chandrika*; I had seen him bent double getting it perfect.

'What do you think?' Veerappan was looking at the sari and me. His eyes were red from not having slept. He worked through the nights by the light of the clay oil lamp kept at some distance from the loom.

'It is a world with the ocean and waves with fish, and sea lions, and boats…and words that dance with my name! It's so beautiful, Appa,' I said and burst out crying.

A few days passed and one of the weavers came running to Veerappan and summoned him to the 'big house' where the zamindar landlord stayed with his family when they visited Seeraivakkam. They lived in the city of Madras. It could mean one of two things: either that Veerappan was going to get a scolding, or an instruction that he would have to pass on to the other weavers.

All the weavers started running toward the Zamindar's house. They looked exactly like the stick figures woven into saris. They assembled by shuffling into a semi-circle, making sure they didn't step onto the verandah. In the verandah, Military Sir was sitting with his red coat and his brass buttons blazing like Amman's ear studs. He had his boots on. All the villagers had their heads bowed and folded palms out of respect to the Zamindar and his family. Military Sir kept saying: 'come on, come on! We haven't got all day in this heat!' I think he meant to be welcoming, but it sounded like a threat. He looked red and was sweating profusely in his coat.

The Zamindar cleared his throat. From the many folds of his neck and chins and layers of gold chains, his voice emerged. 'Veerappan, in this village that is blessed by my father's fathers, this earth that has blessed you with life, and the privilege of craftsmanship, we commend you. From the silk thread we gave you, you created poetry for us.' Then, barely moving his head, his eyes turned to Military Sir to acknowledge his presence, while he continued talking to us in Tamil. 'These outsiders, who wear cloth that does not suit our climate, have shown wonder at your skill. This sari presented to Military Sir will be sent to the temple to adorn Amman. Let your craft lead you to victory over all the vicissitudes of life.'

He raised his right arm and Secretary Sir Aiya came grinning into our view, not unlike a Jackal, shaking his head from side to side as he walked. Secretary Sir held a silver tray with a cloth on it. Zamindar landlord held the sari with my name. It was folded neatly, its gold tassles gleaming in a row like flames.

Military Sir tapped his horsewhip against his boot. One of his servants came forward with a dish that looked transparent at first. I learned it was called glass. Very fragile. Military Sir stood up and started speaking first to the Zamindar and Secretary Sir Aiya spoke to us in Tamil and we made meaning of what was being said between the three of them. Military Sir found the silk of the sari 'wonderful'. This meant that more such cloth was needed. From now on, the covers for the mattress cushions for the Coromandel ebony settees would be covered in silk. There would be no need for patterns or motifs, just the colour that the silk was dyed in.

The gift sari was unfolded and its kingfisher blue began to reflect on the precious glass dish. Everyone was listening, and looked at the sari mesmerized. I caught its reflection on the glass and felt the lightness of a bird in flight. We continued to be talked at by Secretary Sir Aiya and understood that even the looms would have to be remade, as the width of the sari was different from the measurement of the cloth needed to cover the mattress and cushion covers.

'Veerappan!' Secretary Sir Aiya called. 'We have decided that, you will, from now on, weave saris for our illustrious Zamindar's family and for weddings. You will instruct your men to double the amount that is woven for mattress covers. Remember the more we weave, the more prosperous our Seeraivakkam becomes.' He ended, anticipating applause or indeed cheers at the prospect of prosperity. Instead, there was a bewildered silence from the gathering, sensing change.

The Zamindar called out, 'Veerappan, my daughter wants a sari that will live beyond our time. Let it forever be known as that sari from Seeraivakkam. Make sure it is as grand as if it were for Amman, and make sure you have it ready when I ask for it. Measure how much silk thread we need, and the gold of course, and tell Secretary. But first we will give you some thread to start on. You have done Seeraivakkam a service. Make sure the others work hard on the other cloth.'

I saw Veerappan listening attentively. He was holding back the tears from the sheer relief of completion. He had woven all nine yards of the sari. He had created a composition of colours with kingfisher blue shot with the aquamarine blue of the mid-day sea. The poetry of his design had entered the world with words; my name concealed. In his heart he knew these men who made gifts of cloth had no understanding of the love of its labour or its aesthetic. He sighed, probably thanking Amman. His eyes were red. His breathing very short. I knew from his look, which combined fulfilment about his craft with fear—like he was concealing a secret, almost as if he had escaped punishment by sheer luck.

The Zamindar's servant was summoned and he handed a large cloth bag that had threads the colour of sunset and pomegranate peeping out from the opening at the top. The Zamindar stepped down from the verandah and handed the cloth bag to Veerappan with an urgent instruction: 'My daughter's wedding sari. Create it'. Veerappan received it with both hands.

Military Sir smiled jollily and said 'Vee-pun, *you* saris, *they* long cloth, is that clear?'

We both nodded and the other villagers followed us.

When we all walked back in silence together, I was muddled about how many weddings and festival saris had to be done, and would that be by Veerappan alone? I vowed to Amman in my heart that I would work night and day by his side helping with the warp to get the wedding sari, at least, done in time.

When we returned to our hut, and all the other weavers had left, Veerappan took me to a dark corner of the kitchen. Then looking over his shoulder to make sure no one was waiting outside, he looked at me intensely. It hit me in the stomach. Then he held my head and whispered: 'Chandrika, your name...on the sari... If anyone asks about it—can you keep a secret? It is now a pattern. Not your name. Only a pattern.' I saw in my mind's eye *chandrikachandrikachandrikachandrikachandrika* repeated enough times for it to lose meaning or the sense of my name, so that it was 'a pattern'. I nodded vigorously.

What Veerappan had done was to use my name as a signature, changing the history of patterns woven in Seeraivakkam over the previous three hundred years. My name had entered the realm of the gods. I did not know it then, but it could cost him his life. It was his act of rebellion, to use the thread and create a signature of local living names and temple symbols embedded in the design. It was his belief when sober or drunk, that the goddess did not show preference to courtier, king or outcaste. That was her blessing. The sari was also a tapestry of time and the history of our people.

Not a Dream

Two months passed and the season had changed. It was approaching Chitarai masam; the heat of the sun was relentless. The wooden frame for the loom was dry. The floor in the house could not be doused with water for us to feel cooler; the warp threads would lose their tension. Veerappan had taught me how to assist in the warp, but I needed years of bending my fingers to make it perfect. The weft, with the pomegranate-coloured thread, had begun and the sari border was emerging. In his drawings you could clearly see the panels with temple spires interspersed with rudraksh circles and the plantain clusters. At the pallu, the goddess Amman was seated with ten arms holding a sickle, rosary, trident, spear, to protect us from rats and snakes. This was a wedding sari for the Zamindar's daughter. It would be offered to Amman first.

There was a pattern to the days—wake early, light the dried dung cakes to start the cooking fire, then draw water from the well. Once the rice and vegetables were in the earthen cooking pot, I would go and assist Veerappan at his weaving. All along my neck and forearms I started getting a rash. So after a few weeks, Veerappan decided I should only do cooking, and not weaving, till the rash subsided. I applied turmeric paste so the skin would stop

weeping from the blisters. It would of course stain the
threads if I worked on them so I made sure I did not go
anywhere near the loom.

One afternoon, as it happened, I had served
Veerappan his afternoon meal of rice and tamarind
rasam. After disposing the leaf plate to be eaten by the
crows and grazing cows, I returned indoors. Veerappan
went outside to wash his hands and rinse his mouth. I
heard voices. It was definitely Secretary Sir Aiya. There
were two other men from another village. One was burly
and the other wiry. The talismans and tattoos on their
arms were different from ours, as I saw through the
palmyra-shuttered kitchen window. I crept closer.

'Dai Veerappan! What da, got too big for us eh?' one
of the men said.

'Hasn't Sir told you *not* to weave the temple spires on
the border of long cloth?' the other barked.

'I was commissioned to weave the daughter's wedding
sari. It will be blessed in Amman's temple. We have always
woven temple spires. Why should it not be woven now?'
Veerappan was calm. He was stating a fact.

Secretary Sir Aiya decided to use his authority. 'I told
you the red coats don't like it. They are giving us orders
for more weaving and we are giving you more thread...'

'But this isn't the long cloth for covers! This is going
to be Zamindar's daughter's wedding sari...' Veerappan
tried to explain.

'Yes, but, we also inspected the design for the border
of the long cloth from the other weavers. There is a
rudraksha between the temple spires. What is the
meaning of that, eh? We ordered only plain-coloured
silk for the red coats. What do you think you are doing?'

Veerappan sighed. 'The rudraksh is one hand—five fingers width—between each temple spire. It is a measure of the width of the dye on the yarn, and the spires are a marker of how many lengths need to be woven. That is all.'

'We must not alert suspicion that you have other... feelings', Secretary Sir said firmly.

'We are all born of this earth. Our language is our mother; the weaving was given to us by our fathers who were devoted to Amman. We measure and create the symbols we weave from the world around us. Rudraksh, temple spire, lion, peacock...'

'Besh! Besh! Very nice speech Veerappan. If I catch you teaching that to the others everything you have will be destroyed. The red coats think and know your lion, temple spire, rudraksh are a way of inciting others to weave the same symbols, because they are sacred. That way the European will not buy our silk. This is a time of change Veerappan. The gods will survive if we have money to spend on them. You think the sacred cloths have any value? Don't be a fool, Veerappan. The red coats don't want trouble to spread; they know all you weavers are one people. Don't make trouble where we want to make business...'

'But, we *are* one people. The sacred symbols are our stories handed to us by our ancestors. They are the veins through which our looms sing and the threads dance because they keep alive Amman's force. Every festival, people have bought our woven cloth, which brings in money. Why do we have to forget our symbols? Why are we stoking the fire of greed? These red coats think differently from us. They keep moving. There is no bond with the earth and Amman. Besides, the Zamindar did not call me to the Big House to complain. He himself asked me to create Amman's story on his daughter's wedding sari. Why not ask him then?'

Veerappan sounded firm and this threw Secretary Sir Aiya into a state. He started twitching his lips and growing alarmingly breathless and purple in the face. 'How dare you! Do you know who I am? I am a Tiger da! I'll show you my stripes. Who do you think you are, eh? Low caste idiot! Don't even know who your father is and talking back to me, eh?! What arrogance, talking to me about Zamindar's order! First trying to teach me about weaving, and now trying to threaten me, eh?' He was so furious he was choking over his own spittle. Then he looked at the men who had accompanied him. 'Teach him a lesson that he can remember. Silence him if you have to, but don't break his hands...' I heard his sandals grate away against the rubble on the track.

The burly man struck Veerappan on the head with his scythe. Blood spurted and Veerappan fell to the ground. I screamed behind the shutter. They saw me as they scrambled away shouting 'Veerappan! Jagruti! Be warned. It doesn't take much to fan a fire that has started!'

When I ran out to Veerappan, he was face down on the ground, bleeding from the head where the scythe had struck. He had smashed his teeth in and his lip was torn. I realized how bony he was as I tried to lift him. His legs were tangled with shock, and when I tried to raise an alarm he insisted I should not do so. He held on to the broken wall of the well and raised himself. Then, leaning on me, cupped his hand into the clay water pot nearby and washed off the blood before dragging himself back to the loom. He was strong, but his spirit had been struck.

That evening when I lit the house lamp, I prayed to Amman. The owl was hooting earlier than usual. Thinking it was a good omen I decided to look out for its white wings sailing past the mango grove. I went to the edge of our rickety pathway as the dark encircled me in a mist of mosquitoes. I caught sight of the owl winging its way to the next grove. I was so happy. I knew everything would be all right and Veerappan would get better.

There was the thud of a mango behind me, and a flurry of unseen parrots screeched as they scattered. Suddenly I felt a hand on my mouth, a vice-like grip lifted my legs off the ground and as I was blindfolded my hands were tied with short coir. I remember the smell of the jute sack as it was pulled over me and I was carried past our hut. If anyone saw anything it must have looked like men carrying a sack of vegetables over their shoulders.

The blindfold was tight enough for my eyes to be squashed into pulp, and the rough coir rope around my wrists was cutting in with every step they took. I could smell the tartness of mangoes as they stopped and heaved me into a cart. The cart moved fast enough past our cluster of huts in Seeraivakkam. The sound of the bullock's bells and the rising smell of clay as the breeze blew told me we were close to the river and that I was being taken away. The fear that fluttered as I felt everything sinking inside me, made me pass out.

I woke with the smell of urine and the warmth of it running down my legs. I still couldn't see as I was blindfolded, but the sack had been removed and my wrists prickled with the blood tracks around them. I felt the sun and the breeze. I had been dumped on the track and there was no sound of cart or bullocks. It must have been late morning. I heard footsteps—with anklets—walking towards me. Then silence. Goats were bleating in the distance.

'Aiyiyo!' A woman's voice. She splashed some water over me and would not stop talking till she cut through the rope tying my wrists with her sickle. I dared not suggest I preferred having my blindfold removed first. She did remove it eventually. I could only see black rings around everything—the bush, the woman's face. I tried rubbing my eyes with my free fist and she seized my fists and smacked it the way I had seen mothers do it to their daughters when they itched their eyes.

'You are a child in a woman's body. Who did this to you? Aiyiyo! Blood, round your wrists, face, waist. Come, I'll wash you.'

So there in mid-morning light by the pond with the buffaloes and the purple water hyacinths she washed me, as a mother would, round the ears, massaging my hair with a little coconut oil. She took out a small pouch from her waist and gave me some hemp seeds and then put three balls of jaggery rolled with puffed rice in my palm, the kind we used to save for the temple elephants. It was the most delicious thing I had tasted, as I had no idea when I had last eaten. I knew this must be a messenger of Amman. Who else would look after me like that!

We didn't speak the same Tamil, but we understood each other combining facial expressions and hand gestures, sometimes with a comic effect when we had assumed the opposite of what was said.

I must have been taken very far away from

Seeraivakkam and dumped, possibly for dead. What now? I almost wished I had not come to my senses. All I remembered was the owl and Veerappan. And then the smell of sweat, being gagged and blindfolded, the sack, and the smell of clay rising from a river. I suddenly felt a craving for the fish from the river. I stared ahead and apart from the woman who was washing her sari and the two water buffaloes cooling themselves in the pond where I had just been washed, there was nothing to tell me of where I came from and what I must have been. The pavadai half-sari I had on was stained and torn. The woman gave me one of her saris that I wore eagerly to forget my shame.

Had I been taken away because I overheard 'the business'? 'The business' meant money. I had never seen money. But I knew it was costing us our lives.

The woman had a palmyra thatch strung over four uneven bamboo poles as a shelter, hidden by the steep bank of the pond where I had been dumped. Over the next few weeks, as I healed in silence, I understood the rhythms of her day. When she left in the morning I hid in her shelter and gathered drift and rubble with the buffalo dung and made a fire to cook the rice or vegetables she had brought the night before. When she returned in the evenings, the sun would be falling like a red watermelon cut open against the cowdust haze. She lived and spoke in monologues with long intervals of silence. That was a relief, because the effort in understanding what she occasionally said started my head pounding. She had bundles of bark and twigs from which she made pastes and applied some on my wrists and my lip, which had been split open. Whatever she offered to eat or drink I ate without questioning. I was so grateful to be looked after. This could only be Amman. At night with and without the moon, she and I would watch the sky in silence.

The woman's pastes worked on my wrists. There was only a tiny scar left on my right wrist. My cracked lip had healed and my eyelids did not feel the pain or heaviness. The days passed, with my counting how each part of my body was healing, and how my soul was churning. I sometimes felt I had died and I had come to a place where Amman was looking after me before my soul finally found another life. There was no one else that I saw other than this woman, and the water buffaloes—who were definitely the mascots of Yama, the god of death.

Would Veerappan be looking for me? How could he? He was battered and bed-ridden. Would the other weavers have noticed I was missing and raised an alarm? Or would they too have remained silent like on the night of my birth? I longed to see Veerappan and cook him a decent meal, as now my host had taught me new dishes. I longed to go back, in spite of enjoying the care and attention this woman gave me. She taught me some rhymes while we salted the fish to dry and how to count with cowrie shells. I kept dung cakes smoking to keep the crows from swooping down and stealing the fish.

One morning, the sun was just breaking through some rain clouds and the sky was grey blue with crimson and gold slashes. The crows were wildly climbing the sky and you could hear them announcing the day. The woman was standing at the high bank of the pond. She held out her hand as if to call me. I hesitated, and then she turned and smiled calling me to her. I had never explored the other side of the bank before, as I was terrified that I would be discovered, or attacked by wild animals.

I scrambled up to the high bank and holding her hand looked out at the view. We were so far away from anywhere. In the distance there were some palm trees. The riverbed that snaked along the land was nearly dry. But you could see how wide and full it would be in the monsoon. Some cows and herdsman were dotted in the distance. The air was cool and fresh. The woman had two baskets by her side. One with beads and cowrie shells, and the other with bangles. She handed me the basket with bangles and beckoned me to follow her.

It was a long walk down the high bank of the pond to the riverbed. There the ground was soft. We walked without talking. The wind tousled our sun-bleached hair and the baskets creaking on our hips and heads created a rhythm. We approached a field where people were slowly gathering. Cows, bulls, goats, buffaloes, were being tied to tree stumps. An elephant was showering itself with water from a bucket and people were ducking from its spray. A baby elephant was rolling in the sand. A man was arranging many sieves of plantains in a row.

There were many Kuruvanji gypsy men and women strutting around, looking for the perfect spot to sell their wares. Unlike others who had carts or stalls on wheels, which were brightly painted and had blue, orange and green streamers bobbing from them, the Kuruvanji had their well-oiled bodies, with tattoos and silver jewellery and long necklaces of glass beads to attract buyers yet to assemble. They were rolling out strings of many different sized beads from spools of neem twigs. Some beads were the size of pin heads and the others the size of an orange. The string of beads were unspun from their spools and laid on the ground under a shady peepul tree.

I stood entranced, watching a woman combing hair that was so burnt by the sun it was gold. Her three children were around her, scratching their heads. Two other women were setting up a small dung fire to start the meal for about fifteen of them. A big bandicoot was stripped of fur and flesh, ready to be cooked. The men were setting out the birdcages and two had live parrots. I knew they would soon be used for the fortune telling. There were also toys made from scraps of cloth tightly wound into tigers, elephants, and bears; little wooden and clay toys of carts and drums and pipe whistles.

'You are still a child in a woman's body!' said the woman who had brought me. She was talking to the other Kuruvanji; they all laughed welcomingly, without covering their mouths, showing their brilliant white teeth. They gave me some green mango cut in the shape of a chameleon's head dress and it was doused with red chilli, salt and lime. Sucking it made me feel very alive.

I decided to call the woman who brought me 'Akka', or older sister. The Kuruvanji were well travelled and could understand my Tamil and translated it to Akka.

The sun was shifting and soon the early morning would be over. The cattle buyers and villagers who were celebrating the full moon event of the season were beginning to gather. The big drums started pounding and the horns and pipes at the far end of the field announced that the fair was beginning.

This was the first time in my life I could be a child. I went to all the stalls and as Akka was with me, she talked to everyone who offered us a little food in leaf plates or directly in our palms to taste. Tamarind water, lime pickle, mango, pappadums, sticky jaggery toffee, and so much more, I didn't think it would ever stop. Akka sold some beads and bartered for cloth with another buyer. She tied it on me and named it my 'new' sari. I wept at her goodness. She squeezed the tears out of my face and pinched my cheeks as she cried herself. We both knew we had found each other and we were going to be happy for the whole day and the rest of my life. Veerappan would meet her too.

We stood and watched how the cattle buyers tested the bulls by pressing their tails, humps, and hooves. The cows were adorned with red vermillion dots. One man refused to do anything else other than place the cow he had brought in the centre of a circle he had marked with white rice powder. Then he placed little heaps of marigolds north, south, east and west of the circle. On a leaf plate he had laid out peels of oranges, and little yellow 'worship' plantains. He then placed a jasmine garland around the cow's neck. The cow was decked with vermillion and turmeric dots on her forehead, her tiny horns had been painted and strung with strings of beads. She had anklets on her hooves, and her tail had a red ribbon tied to it. As people passed they laughed, partly mocking the man as mad. But he certainly made all of us stop at least for a moment before some would pass on. He was so acrobatic, the way he would dive onto the ground and offer the cow his salutations. Then he brought out a brass plate and placed a betel nut leaf on which he pressed a tiny mound of camphor powder. He lit the camphor from a small flaming torch stuck in the eastern mound of marigolds that was within the circle. He then rang a hand bell the way the temple priests do. He waved the plate with the flame in steady clockwise circles around the cow. Everyone was struck by his clear voice that rang out 'Aum'. He then placed the brass plate with the camphor flame at the edge of the circle facing the cow and then sat cross-legged to the right of the cow at her hooves. She put her right hoof on his right knee. There was a wave of applause and then people began trickling toward the brass plate, making offerings of copper coins, food, cloth, sacks of grain. The man had cunningly made his future on our faith.

By evening, Akka said we could sleep by the riverbank where the Kuruvanji would be. I was frightened and thrilled at being able to sleep under the stars and watch the moon rising, low and gold at first. Lots of villagers who had gathered here from far-off places would be doing the same.

My eyes had seen so much at the fair that my lids drooped unwillingly. I so wanted to see the stars overhead. As I lay down looking up at the upturned bowl of sky, the silhouettes of palmyra and coconut palms encircled it. The temperate earth sighed beneath my spine. It was the first time in my life I smiled in my heart and felt as cared for as in Veerappan's home. The cool breeze, the smell of clay with the scent of fish from the river blew on my face.

Everyone was exhausted as I was, and happy. I fell fast asleep.

The earth began to tremble and I woke to the sound of screaming and the smell of burning flesh.

This was not a dream.

A Misunderstanding

I woke to a blaze of heat and a tide of rising flames. Screaming humans and animals and the stench of burning flesh. There was a child sitting within my reach that had been spared. Its mother's pleading eyes and mouth still open, with arm outstretched, were hacked in two. There were men in coats and bare-bodied men; you couldn't make out their colour or caste as the fire, the colour of molten gold, was glowering behind them. It was an endless fresco of one body gripping on to another, limbed or limbless. Bodies killing, or being dragged to shelter, or blinded; bayonets held like torches gouging and spewing entrails. The horses were frothing and neighing as the bulls and cows were also forming a stampede. I felt the earth rumble. The rising dust clouds dimmed the blaze of the fire but it was a gnashing, and slicing of blades and muskets plunging into everything within reach.

I could neither sit, stand, walk nor run. My legs were the weight of wet wood. I collapsed into a stump and rolled over the sharp stone and scrub toward the clay side of the riverbank. The tide was low, so I slipped into the water. Suddenly I felt my hair being pulled and a horseman dragged me out of the water. I screamed and as the red-coated horseman bent to pull me up. I heard a shot. The horseman grunted and his back lurched over the galloping horse. I heaved myself up by the stirrup, tucking my legs like a bird in flight, and grabbed at the saddle. I used his dead body as a shield. The blood spewing from his mouth covered my face as the horse thundered through the chaos.

We must have travelled far away, as the cacophony dimmed behind us and the blood crusted on my face. I wanted to tear at my face, but my hands had gripped the horse's mane for a lease on life, however short or long. I had never known an animal with such speed when I heard the thundering hooves of another horse behind me. The horse I was on was then steered by another horseman in pursuit of the dead man.

I still couldn't see as the blood caked over my eyes, and I was convinced I was blind. The foaming neck of the horse prompted me to think about breathing and living. Soon, the animal dropped its thundering pace and it cantered till we stopped. It was pitch dark ahead, with the haze of light behind us. The other horseman dismounted and drew out a small lantern he was carrying and lit it. I could see from its pale light he had on the red coat of the English military. More panic. He cut down the body of the dead horseman I was shielded under. I must have looked like a lump of cloth as I was crouched over the saddle and clinging like another dead body, but when he felt my arm he wrenched me off and I tumbled to the ground.

'What the devil! Are you man or beast?' he bellowed.

I crumbled in a deluge of tears, which helped wash some of the crusted blood around my eyes. From the light in the distance, I could see who the dead man was and gasped, 'Military Sir Aiya!' I could see the fires like pinheads blazing behind him.

The Red Coat pulled at my hair. 'Did you know this man? Did you kill him?' The man asked me making the gesture of stabbing. My saliva hung from the sides of my gaping mouth like a drawbridge. Crying helped me breathe through my mouth as my nose was blocked. I just cried and howled, bayed, spluttered, coughed and continued sobbing. He held me very firmly until I grew motionless. It must have been for a while, because we were still standing as the fires in the distance died down. Then the man took out a black cloth from under the saddle of the horse I was on. He stretched out the slumped body of Military Sir Aiya, straightened the limbs and covered it. He let both horses stray at a short distance from us. It was dark enough for us to be hidden, but light would be breaking in the sky soon.

A wagon made from a covered bullock cart was about to pass the track by the clump of trees we were amongst. I dreaded being captured and returned to the market fair; I did not know whether to run away or stay. Akka and the Kuravanji would certainly be dead. What was to happen now?

As the wagon approached, from the rear a soldier stuck his head out. His face was darkened with soot and smoke. He let out a low whistle and the horses came galloping. The man who was with me darted out of the shadows and stood in the track of the approaching wagon. It stopped and the soot-smeared man jumped out from the back and they made hand signals. I was bundled into the back of the wagon, which smelt of tobacco. The horseman carried Military Sir Aiya's body too into the back. The soot-smeared man got onto the other horse and the two horsemen accompanied the wagon front and rear.

Over every stone that the wooden wheels of the wagon turned, it seemed as if Military Sir Aiya's knee, jaw or wrist jumped to life. I sat the entire journey with my ears and head crouched between my knees. I passed urine frequently between gaps in the wood slats of the wagon.

Well past sunrise, we passed a village that looked deserted. Perched within the wagon I was able to peep out. The tracks started looking familiar, winding past the cashew grove and then the mulberry trees. Then we passed a hamlet of huts all burned down. My heart was beating wildly. The milestone that marked Seeraivakkam was stained in blood. There was Veerappan's hut, the tiles of the roof where the loom was kept, the thatch all burned. The horsemen were walking the horses and engrossed in talking. I jumped out of the wagon and ran into the ruins of the hut I knew with my eyes closed. But one of the men had caught up with me. I looked up at the mango tree, and Veerappan was hanging.

All I kept repeating in a language the man who held me by my elbows could not understand was 'why, o why, why...am I being made to see all this?' I was about nine years old, with no words to understand horror or grief. I could not, nor will ever know why humans suffer and cause suffering when they know it cuts deeper than any weapon can.

Something told me that humanity comes in various forms. Here I was, on the ground that was once my home, an orphan. Yet, I was being comforted by a person I did not know. He had all the capability of cruelty, but at this moment he was moved to show me sympathy. He let me hold on to him, kicking and crying. The soot-covered man cut Veerappan's body down. The only thing that steadied my shaking was the belief that Veerappan's soul was crying out for his body's cremation. I gathered the broken dung-cakes that were drying along the low wall of the well behind the kitchen. From the few dried branches that were left by the side of the house the men helped me make a stretcher. We laid Veerappan's body in the frame. I straightened his head along his spine, then aligned his feet and tied his toes together with a string of banana pith. I looked at his hands, the long oval nails, and the index and middle fingers stained with burns and the tobacco he smoked. His neck was strung with a turmeric-yellow thread. The pail with cow urine in which the thread had been soaked for its colour was still half full. I placed his coral-coloured palms encased on his coffee-bean-brown chest. I gathered some dry leaves and laid them over his body to make a pyre. There was no oil. The man with the soot-smeared face looked at me and poured some rum from his flask on the dung cakes that were placed around the body. A fire was lit.

I prayed and prayed so hard, thanking Veerappan for all that he was for me, and that I would never forget his art as long as I lived. The flames from the pyre stung my eyes. I saw his feet melt apart as the pith string dissolved. The flames from the crackling fire melted flesh, and you could hear his bones popping.

The men decided to bury Military Sir Aiya's body here, too, as taking the corpse anywhere in this heat would definitely kill all of us. The stench and the flies that surrounded the covered body could attract vultures and kites. We, the living, would have made a feast for these predators too! As the men were digging a grave, I decided to wash in the small pond by Amman's temple.

Now that I was 'home' I thought I might as well get a clean cloth to wear. All the villagers had fled, their houses derelict and burned.

Something kept calling me to the interior of Veerappan's house. The beams had crashed in, the terracotta tiles broken, but I managed to squeeze in through a side window where the wooden frame had caved in. It was the room with the loom.

The sun was very bright outside and cast sharp rays into the dark, low interior. I must have grown taller since the day I was kidnapped. In spite of the rubble from the pillage, I could see where the loom was. A partly woven sari was splattered with dead embers from the fire, but it seemed to rest like a protective canopy over the loom. I hugged it as if it was Veerappan. He was the one person I knew all my life who knew me, till I was taken away. Who did this? Was it Secretary Sir Aiya's men? Was it the Red Coats? Why burn the whole village? What power made me return this way? Was it Amman who made sure that I performed Veerappan's last rites, even if I was a girl? Only sons could take that on. But in this time of horror there was no time to think of prescribed rituals; there was not even oil to pour over his pyre. It was the dawning of a new age of pouring rum as libation onto the pyre. The important thing was that I could take Veerappan's blessing, even if he was dead. I had woven his secret of weaving my name in the sari into my memory. I prayed to Amman that his soul would pass through the gateposts of rest before he took on the body of something else.

I removed the burnt half-woven sari from the loom. It peeled away in parts like a snake's shed skin. Under the trestle of the loom I saw the rusty trunk in which

Veerappan stored skeins of thread that were blessed at
the Amman shrine before he started weaving new cloth.

The lock had been broken open and inside it
under the large bobbins, was a sari. The gold tassels
glimmering, revealed an unforgotten story. My cindered
hands trembled as I took it out. The sari's body was
pomegranate-pink, with the sunset orange border
interwoven with gold. Its weight was sumptuous. I dared
not rub my blood-stained face into it. Tears again. But
this time of joy. A message across the world of the dead
to the living. Amman was the only chord of hope and had
drawn me here. I held the sari as carefully as I could. In
the centre of the pallu, Amman had been woven, seated,
with six arms, and in two of them she held spools and
yarn. The others had sugarcane, a scythe, and a folded
cloth. The sacred rudraksh beads, the temple spires,
were interspersed to form the square frame enclosing
Amman. Underneath her figure was a thin yellow silk
thread signature in Tamil, *S. Veerappan*. The background
of her pandal where she was seated, had vertical ripples
of *chandrikachandrikachandrikachandrika* like strings of
jasmine. Can you imagine? He had made me, an orphan,
immortal by weaving my name in the wedding sari of the
Zamindar's daughter! He had created his design to be
followed for generations and my name would be echoed
throughout the known world in silk in the safe-keeping
of Amman. I thought I'd die of happiness if I lingered any
longer. When I looked at the edge of the sari, it looked
as if it had been burned with an open flame to separate
a section of it. The sari seemed complete, but it was only
nine yards. I knew Veerappan had been commissioned by
the Zamindar to weave twelve yards as the wedding sari

for his daughter. Time was too short for that ambition. Was the Zamindar and his family safe? Had the wedding happened? I didn't need to know. Time had turned another page.

I found Veerappan's head cloth coiled by the side and wrapped the sari in it. I looked in the niche and there were his dhotis. I took them. I found hope.

As I came out of the ruins, the men were lowering Military Sir Aiya's body into the grave, and shovelling the earth with two large spades. I don't know why, but I felt I could trust them. They had not killed me yet, Amman had brought all of us here, and who knows where we would be taken. I signalled to them that I was only going to wash in the pond.

I washed in Seeraivakkam's pond, deserted of its buffaloes, children, and women slapping the black stone to wash the clothes. The blood and dirt from my nails took some scrubbing and, having scraped myself with the rough stones, I felt like a human being. My hair was almost matted. Fortunately, the soap nut tree where we villagers used to wash had scattered its fruit on the ground. It was plenty for me to lather the dried blood out of my scalp. I took Veerappan's dhoti and wrapped it around my upper and lower body like a tunic, as I had nothing else. Clean, and cleansed, I clutched the wedding sari of the Zamindar's daughter wrapped in Veerappan's head cloth and went to the Amman shrine. The lean-to was burned. Nandi, the old black stone bull, sat facing the shrine, teaching us that no time is too long to wait for insight. The hanging brass lamps were stolen, and black stains of camphor burnt out on the floor reminded me of the time it was busy. The turmeric triangle bordered with red vermillion now looked like broken words from a language that had been put to sleep.

Only the black stone figure of Amman in a sari with purple, yellow, red and green checks and gold border was a witness to all that had happened. I undid that sari to wear the next day. I held the chandrika sari in my hands as an offering to the shrine of Amman. No oil for the lamps, once flowing with devotion. I prayed to Amman for strength to give me courage to walk this battlefield of life. I was so absorbed in my prayer that I did what I would normally do, reach blindly for the rope to ring the temple bell. I heard footsteps behind me. It was the first horseman who had run up the steps of the temple to hold the bell to stop it from resounding. He gestured that it would raise an alarm—after all for him and his comrade this was enemy country. I must have looked at him with such disdain, even superiority, that he staggered to his knees as if offering salutation to Amman. I saw from his crooked smile it was mock prayer. He looked at me and said: 'Edward.'

'Ed wood', I replied, and holding my head high, with the sari in my hands, did my perambulations round the temple, as a temple priest would. He watched me doing three rounds, and while I continued to go on another six, he stripped his coat and went to swim stark naked in the pond, his white chest gleaming under his red face.

I found some rice and lentils in the Amman temple larder and cooked it. Edward and the soot-smeared horseman, who was very pale once he had washed himself, were restless and waiting like two dogs for their leaf-plate of rice and sambar. While I was not their hostage, they were made captive by my cooking. Even if they had held me as ransom, it was better to stay with them as in any case I had nowhere to go. They were waiting for a caravan they said. That would buy my passage safely across the next many days of travel, as we had to keep moving.

I didn't know where we were traveling, but one night when we camped, another bullock cart came and out of it tumbled nine musicians. The woman of the group sang for us and we shared food that I had never tasted before. There were rotis and pickle made from carrots, radish and brinjal that they had travelled with from the north. Her voice was deep and over three nights she taught me songs of waiting, protest, and women's friendship in a language called Dakhni. She taught me how to make paan from betel nut leaves different from the way it was offered at Amman's shrine. She also taught me to wear kaajal in my eyes. She made me smell her collection of different kinds of attar for different seasons, dressed flowers in my hair and showed me how to tie a full sari in a style that she kept referring to as 'hamare mein', that I took to mean her people. The seventh day they were gone, without a trace. I had the song she taught me embedded in my heart.

Under the stars, Edward held what looked like a small brown box in his hands. But the box was not made of wood; not the kind of story-box Storytellers carried and opened when they travelled through Seeraivakkam. The one Edward held out was made of leather. I felt the texture and smelled it. It smelled of Edward's hands and the reins of the horses. I smoothed my hands over it and it felt harder but similar to the leather puppets of the tholabommalatu that used to come around festival times each year in Seeraivakkam.

'Book', he said. 'Buk', I repeated. 'No, bo-ok', he said

circling his lips the way the carp pouted in the temple
tanks when you fed them rice. I made fish lips and the
sound slipped out 'book', like a bubble of air under water.
Then he opened what looked like a lid to the box, which
had a gold band edging the borders. Inside was a book.
It was the first time I had held one so close. He held
one sheet between his fingers before turning it. 'Page' he
said. 'Pa-ege', I repeated watching intently the shape of
his lips as he made these sounds. That was the first time
little patterns on a page seemed like the patterns that
were woven by Veerappan, and I wanted to know what
it meant.

It was a book and he taught me to read my first word
spelt in English: 'Scheherazade'. It was the first book I
had seen and it had images in it. Then Edward showed
me how his name was spelt in the book. He asked my
name and wrote it in the book. For the first time I saw
how my name looked in English: *Chandrika*. I liked the
dot of the 'i'. It was like the Hindu dot on the forehead.

'It will take you to different worlds,' Edward said when
he pressed the box with the book into my hands the last
time I saw him. Just as I got into a rhythm of cooking
and staring at the patterns on the page by the campfire
at night, the caravan arrived in my life like another
tempest. So many people, so much food, so many rules
and regulations. That was when Mr Whippett first saw
me, and I him. It was decided that I should be given a
religion and sent to the Convent to study. I hugged my
little wooden trunk that Edward had made me, where
I kept the brown leather bookcase, and the black stone
statue of Amman that Akkka, the Kurathai woman, gave
me. I made a bag out of Veerappan's coarse head cloths

and hid the pomegranate-pink sari within a false bottom of the trunk.

At the Convent when I began to read without making much meaning of the words, I soon learned of the 'Indian Mutiny'. In some circles it was described as a war of the natives to oust the English. It was then that I realized the English were not Indian.

I returned to my senses in my room in Grace Hall. I recollected how the Coromandel settee was unwrapped before my very eyes, the mattress covering that was woven by my people from Seeraivakkam, my birthplace.

I felt like Undine, in the painting above the settee, who as a nymph had to take on a soul in a human body. Often I had seen people both in India and in England looking as if they inhabited their bodies, but somehow, their soul was hovering in another geography. I observed this particularly with the dancers at Hindu temples, and the composers in European concert halls. They held a map of thoughts and feelings within and were constantly translating what they contained within them to the public at large through their Art. What a transformation they had undergone, to experience a deep and soulful pasage that was performed for the public, who would possibly never know the arduous interior journey of paring and distilling the essence of imagination in the work! And yet on the exterior, for all purposes, a composer, a dancer, a poet looked as ordinary, even ragged, as everyone else. I was not accomplished in any art or science, neither could I find any talent. The sole virtue I had was the talent to survive. The tumult within my soul had to carry on while I kept calm on the outside.

What flashed vividly in my mind were Veerappan's fingers; his knuckles the size of sambar shallots while creating the letters of my name in a pattern of yellow thread. It was his code of writing a history through symbols of the way a people believed in time and space— the rudraksh for meditative auspiciousness, the peacock for weddings, the goddess Amman for courage to face intruders. His greatest fear, when I look back now, must have been the rise of merchant supremacy displacing the role of art and the artisan. Could the spirit that turned the soil and grew the bark; that fed the silk worm, that spun the thread; that dyed the yarn; that wove the cloth from the colours of the sunrise to the sunset; with all creatures telling their story of how the earth breathes and dies and lives again, be taught or bought by an Order? Who would be left to spin the stories about Amman, time after time, in new ways? It was a tradition he did not want obliterated, and he was willing to give his life for it. Till his end he fought against the supremacy of greed in the name of trade, and the grip of profit above Art. His silent weapon was his craft. He had woven a hidden history to the rhythm of Seeraivakkam's heartbeat.

So many lives, Indians, and those English in India, had been trampled, tormented, blown apart. There was turmoil and confusion about what the hell was being fought for—and all the tea party in the drawing room at Grace Hall could say about the events of 1857 was that *it was a misunderstanding?* It diminished the whole bloody affair to a seeming quarrel between lovers.

For me, it ripped open a purple scar of history I had forced myself to forget.

Bookends

Norfolk, March 1871

Master Stephen was solely interested in engraving and had out all manner of books. He was looking at Naturalist engraver Thomas Bewick's famous cow. Scattered all about him on the vast oak table in the Library were drawings of elephants, camels and water buffaloes from *The Graphic* collection of engravings, to determine the difference between cows bred in England and those in India.

There was an earnest endeavour, on his part, to discover what made the Asiatic or Indian 'holy cows, forbidden by the hindoos to be eaten', even when starvation was rampant during the famine in Orissa. The prospect of different beliefs among people that determined the way familiar objects, and indeed animals, were treated in dissimilar ways across the world had yet to dawn on him. His mind was racing to get acquainted with the differences in species, including human societies, as if he was travelling overseas imminently and would be lost if he did not know how to discern the variations.

Once Master Stephen and Miss Isobel got past All Souls' Night, their discipline waned. After the evening I catalogued as *Misunderstanding of 1857*, I daily withdrew from company after teaching and reading to the children. I decided music was my only source of comfort and diligently worked on 'Amazing Grace' from John Newton's *Olney Hymns* from over a hundred years ago. Thus, I was able to quell the torment of knowing my origins, its history with the country I now lived in, and the patience with which I had to deal with my present surroundings, without coming across as ungrateful to my genuinely beneficent employers.

This was a relief, as I could now focus my attention on music and words from other cultures—delivered through English, but that had meant specific things, and had not been experienced in an English way of thinking. Christmas was quiet, as the Grace family decided to celebrate with friends of the family in Holland, and the New Year in London. I had caught a cold and decided to bide my time at Grace Hall amidst a reduced staff.

On the return of the Graces to their home, this routine of mine was interrupted by Lord Grace's request to ascertain specific words of Arabic origin. I was happy to turn my attention to this, as the words were familiar, but not the same as the Urdu or Hindustani I had encountered during my life as an orphan in the convent in Calcutta. The book placed on my table was *The Arabian Nights Entertainments*.

I smiled to myself as I remembered how the first word I learned to spell in English was *Scheherazade*. And what nearly made me laugh out loud was how Edward, who had taught me how to spell the word in English, kept silent and nodded in affirmation when I asked him if he was the same Edward as the illustrator of the book, Edward Lane.

Although Lord Grace had placed the Calcutta 1 edition on my table, I could decipher the frame of the entire story. The more I read the more I was absorbed. Surely, this was the power of story and the storyteller. How could a woman in an eastern land have the courage to transform the villainy of the Sultan Shahryar, and free the city of the death sentence on virgins? It was a bewitching account of Scheherazade's storytelling that tamed his senses from a position of prejudice to an acknowledgement of reason through wonder. Could I ever do such a thing? Was I educated just to be well-mannered, or were ideas to have an effect on my way of being? What does every human want? Freedom, I told myself. But everywhere, everyone was bound if not in chains, then by the lack, want, or excess of money, and unhappiness. And yet time after time the need for 'civilization' was built on money, driven by acquisition and further invention.

After battling with my wits about what really caused unhappiness, I decided it was prejudice. It clouded reason, stifled compassion and drowned forgiveness. But as with Scheherazade, she taught Shahryar imaginative stories at night; the dark time when the light of the day's routine and reality could be suspended. I marveled at how she paced her storytelling from nightfall to daybreak, each time leaving a question unanswered. The Sultan was left wanting to hear more. In time, night after night of listening against the dense backdrop of darkness, he gave up his prejudice against all women, and from that proceeded his understanding that the violence against them must end. I was so taken that once or twice I loudly exclaimed 'Shabash Scheherazade!' as if she were in front of me and I was in her thrall.

One day Lord Grace informed me that he and a friend were collecting words from various languages that were used in English. 'Coir' from 'kayr' or rope in Tamil, and 'catamaran' from 'kattu maram'—strips of wood tied together with rope—were ones I was quick to recognize. 'Shahar' was city and 'azad' was free—the name of my heroine. Her sister was 'Duniya'—the world, azad—who freed the world. This way I got to read newly translated works in English for my amusement. By March, I was feasting on The Wife of Bath from Chaucer's *Canterbury Tales*. It surprised me that a widow could be so full of life with an insatiable desire for love, and excess.

Lord Grace called me into his Library. There was hail outside and the snowdrops were beaten down. I had never seen Lord Grace so excited, nervous and fumbling. His sleeves were stained with ink as he seemed to be in a flurry of correspondence. Packets of letters were stamped in crimson wax with his seal. They were stacked in neat rows on his vast oak desk. The cameo of Lady Grace seemed to look on benignly at the many compartments of his desk.

'C, thank you for the translations of the words and phrases. I've just heard from the Collector of Words that your efforts have been of "heightened satisfaction" in contributing to what we are planning—to send these on to the Words Committee of The Philological Society, who are endeavouring to put together a new Oxford English Dictionary!'

'An Oxford English Dictionary!'

'Good god! C...you look like you've seen the Archangel! This is really a new English dictionary on historical principles. It's a long way yet. The Committee meets in London. And they've been looking for volunteers from around the colonies to...' he put on his pince nez to locate the sentence as he began reading from the letter he held, '"be assigned particular books, copying passages illustrating word usage onto quotation slips". And where I've been devilishly lucky is to have you right here! Thank you, and congratulations! Have you enjoyed it?'

'More the thanks to you, sir, for the use of your Library.' I was delighted that I was contributing to a larger world of words. Yes, it was English, and I was now in a world where words and phrases even from other languages could be illustrated.

'Let's move on to the next set, shall we? Perhaps you could look at this? For phrases that are possibly used in conversation?' He handed me a deep red leather-bound book. *Thirrukurral*. I knew it by hearing the sound of the title in my head as Tamil, while my eyes were reading it in English. I remembered the pundit at the temple in Seeraivakkam quoting from the author Thiruvalluvar when he went to visit families where a wedding was to take place:

The one who is capable of converting half a coin into a thousand gold coins is a wife, and the one who is capable of reducing a thousand gold coins to half a coin is also a wife.

Aanal (Explanation):
This is why people say marriage is made in heaven. If you have a good wife you have a good fortune, if you have a bad one you are doomed.

All women are good: good for something or good for nothing.

When the eight- and nine-year-old girls like myself, quite often the brides-to-be, were standing in the doorway, he would point his index finger at us, possibly out of good humour and recite, following with an explanation.

> *If the five and the three are at hand, even an ignorant girl can cook.*
> *Aanal:*
> *It is easy to do a thing when one has all the help required.*
> *The 'five' are pepper, salt, mustard, cumin and tamarind. The 'three'*
> *Are water, fire and fuel.*

During my reverie, I was smoothing my hand over the page, with the embossed title in gold letters on the deep red leather cover. I was in another world, revelling in memory, but enthralled that the book of power from which the pundit quoted was now in my hands, and I— that little girl from Seeraivakkam who was not taught to read and write, peeping through the doorway of a marriage house long burned down—would be able to read it. I nearly jumped when Lord Grace said:

'...And as a treat, here's a book that you might enjoy.' It was William Thoreau's *Walden*. I had never heard the title or the name. It was in English, but from a writer in America. America was still a continent I had to discover in my own mind. The only story I associated with America was with a name, Christopher Columbus, and how those natives were called Indians, because he assumed he had arrived in India. The shape of the literary world for me was flat; a shelf with India and America for bookends marking the limits to my knowledge.

Love

Norfolk, April 1873

One morning I awoke and parted the drapes and noticed the light had changed in the wide Norfolk sky. There were grey clouds, but the fingers of sunlight poured down on the grounds and fields the way I had seen handfuls of wheatgrain poured into cooking pots at the time of feasts. In the distance lining the fields there were tall leafless Lombardy poplars bracing the wind. Their branches crowfeet against the sky; a stationary militia about to explode with buds into foliage. Gulls screeched, preparing us well in advance for a storm at sea. The air was lighter and smelled different in spite of the piercing draught. And then I heard it. The skylark. An outburst of love, almost a lament, announcing his availability for a mate.

My heart darted. Spring had arrived. I didn't care how cold it was. The first shoots and bird song were a relief from long dark days and nights with the wind churning up a howl.

Lord and Lady Grace had decided it was time to see the lambing first that day before undertaking an excursion by boat, if the tide was right, to see the grey seal pups by Blakeney point.

The North wind was bitterly cold as we set out

through the avenue of leafless ash and lime trees that semi-circled around Grace Hall and were carefully planted on the swamp lands by Lord Grace's ancestors. We came past the livestock shed, then the barn where an ewe was bleating piteously. Lady Grace urged me to keep Isobel and Master Stephen at bay, as she walked toward the barn to give instructions to assist the birthing.

I could see crocuses straggling along the grassy banks while Isobel and Stephen circled around my arms in a merry dance singing a potted rhyme of an 'Easter Carol', as they called it, that made me laugh out loud. It was about me being their pillar of joy and tower of woe which ended with a boisterous refrain of 'ho, ho ho!' I thought it was just the three of us playing fools when someone interrupted our merriment.

'You must be Miss Chan-dreeka?' I was still in the momentum of convulsing with laughter as Stephen and Isobel took a final turn when I caught sight of a gentleman standing stock still with a top hat that he was holding above his head to 'salute' me. I was startled. An unfamiliar voice called me by my Indian name emphasizing the wrong syllables. My name sounded so unfamiliar, not because of his accent, but because it had never been uttered in England. I was always C to the Graces, and Miss Christina to the entire staff at Grace Hall, as that was my Christian name.

'Jason', he said. My knees were going to give way, I thought, now that Master Stephen and Isobel had stopped. I felt I was still spinning. It was his baritone that resonated in my bones and my head and heart felt loosened from their usual place. 'Jason Melville', he said again, and caught my elbow before I sank in the soft mud.

We heard Finch barking and baying, followed by Lord Grace who was trying to be heard above it. 'Oh! There you are, Jason!' Lord Grace shouted warmly as he turned from the kitchen entrance, out toward us.

'You do waddle like a duck, sir!' Isobel said impishly as she ran to her father navigating the squelching mud track awkwardly in his riding boots. Lord Grace roared with laughter and picked up Isobel in a swoop and she laughed at her father's display of mock anger.

Lady Grace peeped out from the barn, possibly wondering what all the commotion was about. Her aides carried out two blood-smeared newborn lambs in a wheelbarrow as quickly and discreetly as they could. Master Stephen stood close to me, holding my waist after I had regained my stance.

'I see you've been swift at introductions,' said Lord Grace as he approached, holding Isobel's hand.

'Well, not entirely,' said the gentleman who had introduced himself as Jason Melville.

'Ah! Miss Christina, may I present Mr Jason Melville, the Convenor of the volunteer committees for words, from the Early English Text Society. Er...that we propose to use to form the Oxford Dictionary?' Lord Grace attempted to conceal his enthusiasm as he looked first to his guest, and then to me, almost seeking our approval.

'How d'you do sir.' I said, thanking my stars that my skin was dark enough to cover the blood rushing to my face.

'I am sorry Jason, old fellow, you do have a habit of popping up at very short notice! I've hardly had time to inform the household', Lord Grace added good-humouredly.

'Well...as you well know travel plans across the Atlantic can be as capricious as the gods, as they're dependent on my newspaper Editors. Miss Chan-dreeka, I am eternally grateful for your attention to all the Indian and Persian words you've assiduously sent on. It has illuminated the collection.' His voice did it again. The foreign timbre with which he spoke in English resonated in my bones.

'Well, well, well, Jason, this time if you don't stay with us long enough, I'll have nothing to say to you anymore!' said Lady Grace, smiling widely as she approached our gathering.

We all ambled back to the main house through the kitchen, which threw Mrs T, the cook, into such a dizzy spell that she nearly fell over Finch. She was caught between wondering whether to curtsey or tell Isobel off for fingering the pear and custard tarts that were being arranged in the hamper for the excursion to Blakeney. She gulped as she saw Finch's flapping jowls slip a salmon finger sandwich down his throat while Isobel 'accidently' dropped a scone off the cake-stand and caught it swiftly, only to eat it, muttering, 'it could not go back on, as that would be ill-mannered.'

The kitchen was steaming, as was the oxtail soup from the large copper pan. Mr Melville chatted with Mrs T and the pantry girls, recognizing that there were new members of staff. Lady Grace introduced each of them. In my period of service that I had been at the Graces, this was the first time I had met Jason Melville, and yet he was familiar with details about the staff. It was apparent that he kept in touch frequently, even if he had not visited.

Jason Melville brought an air of freshness and a

manner that seemed to revive Grace Hall. He was American. I had never met an American before. All I had read from the English papers was that Americans were different. They spoke the language, but it sang, with the inference that it 'sagged'. It was a drawl. They were categorized as a species, implicitly regarded as an amalgam of convicts and runaways struggling to establish a tradition or civilization, in spite of having a constitution and a nation.

But Jason Melville was different. It didn't take me long to gather information about him from the Notes on Contributors to the Philological Society. His informality, the way he took the trouble to say my birth name, was a whole new world to me. Lord and Lady Grace had known him for several years. Jason Melville was a reporter of the American Civil War and was on the side of the Union. He had met Lord Grace at Oxford on one of his trips while engaged in the supervision of the volunteer committees to collate words in the English language derived from the colonies. It was evident that from their mutual curiosity grew a keen intellectual bond and friendship. Both Lord Grace and Jason Melville preserved an independent spirit under a veneer of decorum. Lady Grace made the friendship complete and was awarded the status of free expression on women's views across classes in the company of both gentlemen.

Holding the Thread

The boat trip to see the grey-seal pups was postponed as the tide was too low. It took place two weeks later. This had calmed Mrs T considerably. She feared the finger cakes had been squelched by Isobel's eagerness, the moment she was distracted by Jason's charm and enquiries about her husband and grandchildren. It made Mrs T cry with pride that she worked in a household where the Master and Mistress and their guests were so caring. With a scarcity of handkerchiefs about her person, she resorted to whipping off her bonnet and bellowed her nose into it with a triumph of emotion.

The prospect of preparing for another excursion allowed Mrs T to take into account a new recipe, or 'receipt' as Jason called it. He gave it to Mrs T, saying: 'Can you keep a secret? This is the surprise!' He handed her five pounds of pecan nuts, and a sheet of instructions on how to bake 'Boston Cream Pie'. I was part of the conspiracy to keep it a surprise and translate cooking terms from the American into English for Mrs T.

The day before, in the pantry Jason taught Isobel and introduced Master Stephen to the fine craft of baking as a chemistry lesson. They were taught their first European international treat. 'Here's the original Cookie', he said as he drew it out of the oven and the children looked entranced at the palm-size flat round biscuit with bits of pecan nuts and glazed cherries. And we all had a lesson in pronouncing Cookie, and the original 'Koekie' from Dutch. I was enchanted how a small cake from one continent had traveled and metamorphosed into a popular confection in another continent. Who carried it, how did they get the ingredients, how did it spread? Was it convenience, or shared taste across cultures? While Mulligatawny was adapted to English tastes by adding beef in India, how was it that the curry was difficult to adapt in England?

My brow must have been furrowed as I was absorbed in my thoughts amidst his audience. Suddenly, as he was holding a warm cookie up in the air, he looked at me and gave me such a broad smile. His Abraham Lincoln beard widened around his jaw line and chin and I saw his clear open face; his blue eyes looking directly into my eyes. My heart fluttered. I grew a moustache of perspiration on my upper lip. I felt here was someone who knew me for who I was and wanted me to see him beyond race, difference, status. We were a woman and a man sweeping out a loneliness that paved our lives across continents. We were beyond the world of words now.

When we arrived at Blakeney harbour there were two hours before the boat ride. We found a grassy bank where Mrs T's carefully packed hamper was laid out. We sat down in a circle and the clear orange pekoe tea was poured into the china cups. Jason tapped three times with a spoon on his cup. 'Ladies and Gen'leman! A toast! Here's to the great tradition of English Tea brought to us all the way from the East!' said Jason.

'Ceylon, actually', said Lord Grace to provoke his friend. 'Jason, my man, when will Americans learn that anything east of Europe is made up of individual civilizations, and countries, hmm?'

'Ooh! Well, when will the British learn to stop taxing every consumable or luxury that comes from the...I defer to your correction...India and China?' Jason said with a smile.

'Let's call a truce. Let's drink to the Boston Tea Party shall we? And American Independence?' said Lady Grace between the banter.

'Chandreeka, here's to Indian Independence, some day, huh?' said Jason seconding the toast.

Just a hundred years ago this conversation would not have been exchanged between colonizer and colonist—as the Americans were known. The East India Company had brought on the deluge with its deficit. British taxation meant that the colonists were compelled to buy tea as dictated by the Imperial Government. Finally, in protest, the colonists sank a shipment of East India Company tea in Boston Harbour.

What was happening in India? It was more than policy and taxation. It was about people, known as natives, who were slowly having indigo, then cotton, and then increasingly salt from their own land, taxed and taken away from them to build the buildings of the rich Empire. Each day's lines of newsprint were the black and white stairs of desperation I climbed to face the horror of news: killings, burials, from both sides, and the feeling of leaving behind a people I cared for, but no longer knew.

The men toasted with a quick dram of whiskey while Lady Grace and I had sherry with our orange pekoe tea. Stephen and Isobel raised their steaming hot cocoa poured from the hot bottle by Chastity, the new maid, who had accompanied us.

'I received a letter from Ophelia,' began Lady Grace savouring the aroma of her combined beverages. Ophelia was Lord Grace's younger sister visiting in Boston. 'She thanks you for your introduction to Mr Walt Whitman before she went in search of...'

'A far more healing presence to be in than the man she went looking for, I can assure you,' said Jason. I was given to understand that Ophelia had sailed to North America to meet with Educationists, and those who opposed slavery, so she could gain support against the ill treatment of slaves and trading rights of slave ships. She was also part of the committee of world volunteers of words from the colonies.

'I was charmed by her ability to fight for so many ideas!' said Jason.

'Oh yes, our Ophelia is armed with words. I often wondered why we never named her Joan-of-Bark!' Lord Grace rounded off with a chorus of laughter and then checked himself in defence of his non-conformist sister.

'But coming to the point, Ophelia was retracing Mr Minor's footsteps and his obsession with words—and thanks to him we are having a growing volume of words for the great Oxford.' Of course, Jason meant the Dictionary project.

'The effects of the Civil War on Mr Minor in my opinion are, in a word, colossal. He has a fractured imagination, but it sparks off a dread or fascination for letters of the alphabet and the words they can make—and that, it cannot be denied, is of great use to us.' Jason was pensive. 'It could be the bridge, in later explorations of the mind, between how we look at words as signs, and thread them into language by making meaning of it.'

I'm not sure what came over me, as I was listening attentively, but I sighed, audibly. Everyone's words, the meaning, hung like music. I felt comfortable listening, but could not participate if I were asked to, and yet seemed to understand to what Jason was referring.

The hours passed, the tide was up and the men who came to tug the small boats wore thick knitted sweaters with high knitted socks, and had coarse hands where skin and nails seemed of the same hardness and strength against the cold and the bitter North Sea. Jason helped Lady Grace into the boat, and Master Stephen ensured my dress did not drag in the water when the boat began to sway, tipping from one side to the next. Then with a lunge and a deep well of song, the men pushed the boat into the water. I felt such a release of the past as I looked into the waters dividing as the boat surged ahead, buoyed by the silken waves. I was still standing when it lunged forward and I lost my balance. I fell and Jason caught my waist and seated me safely in the boat. I felt his large, light hands warm against my ribs. I could see the light from the grey and honey-coloured sky reflected on the swelling waves, creating sparkling arcs around the boats, the way fish scales catch the light.

Lord Grace had quickly drawn out his binoculars and was looking at the shingled shore in the distance. Lady Grace had begun her homemade riddles, asking Isobel to complete her iconic references. 'Arion and the…?

'Golden Fleece?' replied Isobel, while Master Stephen couldn't resist his judgment: 'How unfortunate! You must attend to your Classics if you wish to be civilized.'

Lady Grace shook her head. 'No! Think water. Let's
try another one. Who is the Roman goddess of Love?'

The water gurgled and murmured past. It was Spring,
life was bursting all around me. The gulls and terns
flying overhead were free, because in this boat, in this
company, the men did not have guns to shoot the things
they spotted. That was thanks to their good sense in
admitting Lady Grace's opinions and giving weight to
our contributions in all subjects for discussion. I was
reassured that sometimes all adult humans of different
races, religions, sex, could be equal.

I couldn't hold myself back any longer. I held my hands
at my back, ripped off my gloves and plunged a hand
into the water. The waves cut into my skin. It made me
remember, as the water coursed through my palm, about
a time I ran my finger over the golden threads that had
chandrikachandrikachandrikachandrikachandrika running
along the border of a sari and Veerappan had asked me:
'What do you think?' And I had replied:'It is a world with
the ocean and waves with fish, and sea lions, and boats…
and words that dance with my name! It's so beautiful'.

Suddenly I felt something grip my hand, I almost
screamed. I had to be careful not to struggle or raise the
alarm. It was Jason. His hand, too, was like a slab of ice,
and with the friction of both our cold hands under the
rippling waves of water by the side of the boat we felt the
heat of skin and blood, and the wonder of desire.

By his touch I felt I wasn't like Undine. I was human,
and a woman. I had learned to see myself as Other by the
invisible forces that were drawn around me; partly by the
events of history, and partly by the genteel environment
I had been placed in.

The width and depth of Jason's knowledge of nature, politics, philosophy, civilisations, war and humanity seemed to me unfathomable. It was the way he applied it to all mankind as an example of living that made it a reality. It was not what he knew, but his curiosity, and insistence on asking questions. What would have been considered too enthusiastic amongst English and Indian society, in his case seemed a genuine enquiry into the heart of the matter. I deemed it a virtue worth receiving my undying loyalty and love.

'There! Just a few pups. Common grey.' Lord Grace was pointing in the direction of a distant shingled bay. We were some miles in and our rowers were hardy and swift through the soft mist. Lady Grace drew out her binoculars. 'The poor dears. The harbour's too much traffic. Of course it would help if more than half the men who come here wouldn't want to shoot everything to return to their halls with a trophy!'

I kept thinking of Undine, the water nymph in the painting above the Coromandel settee in Grace Hall. I was mesmerized by the water, this feeling of fire in my blood in the midst of water, safety, and the light from the mist defining soft forms by their volume. I felt that all that I needed to know about life was illumined in that soft ring of light of floating forms; the burdens that Undine had to take on to be human.

'Do you know *Sakuntala*?' I thought he said. He murmured it while the sound of the water, the boat, and the Graces' eagerness at spotting the seals drowned our conversation.

'Were you thinking of the ring she loses in the water while making her way to see the King?' I heard myself saying.

Jason continued as if we were forming the same sentence through the same thought, 'Cursed, he cannot remember her without the ring. And then he cannot forget her. When the ring is discovered, it's too late. She has left him. Yes, the ring of remembrance.'

We were so close. We were mist from water. This man, who was the bridge across all the continents of my being.

'So, Chandreeka, what knowledge can you throw to our Stephen and Isobel here on the common grey seal?' he said, in a voice that brought reality back in.

'I wonder,' said Lord Grace, 'how these creatures are different from the ones they call the Weddell seals, who can stay below water for a good hour.'

'All creatures adapt to new worlds—we see the endurance of children to different situations—working in forges, cleaning stables, all dangerous, but adapting.'

On our way back, I tried to keep the threads of all that I was thinking simultaneously. Undine's ring, the mist, and the seal pup were all swimming in the surface of my thoughts.

'What does the Sanskrit "sutra" mean?' Jason said as we were returning in the coach with Stephen and Isobel and Chastity.

'A verse that contains a doctrine', I replied.

'Oh? Even in theatre?'

'If you add "dhara", the keeper of the thread. The Story Teller.' I suddenly found I couldn't stop myself. 'Yes, thread holds the cloth that covers the body. The cloth is the story everyone sees, even believes to be true. But the thread is what holds the entire cloth together; as it does the truth of the story.' I had never expressed what I believed in before.

'Hold the...thread...' Jason was making sense of what I said and was repeating the words slowly, almost to himself.

Meeting Jason Melville nearly three weeks ago had turned my sense of time upside down. My mind was filled with words and ideas and independent thoughts; the speed was exhilarating. I could barely keep up with my routine of teaching the Sunday Classes at St Mary's Church for the orphans without a poem, or an essay rearing up in my head. Isobel began to feel a new enthusiasm toward learning without visiting the kitchen too often. It did help when we studied geography and I decided to use a lot of analogies from baking in describing the layers of the earth as cake crust, fossils and molluscs as ideal soup tureens for individual portions. She weaned herself out of the practice of waiting for tea, and became an able assistant at the Sunday classes in teaching the alphabet with her excellent illustrations of objects.

I was happy. I had never known happiness. I had seen happiness on people's faces—when Lord Grace looked at Lady Grace and she returned his smile. I had seen it on innumerable occasions: singers during a performance; Mrs T when the first lamb roast of Spring came out perfect and the meat slipped off the bone; Chastity when she churned the butter so it came up like a cloud when she held it in her palms; on certain orphans' faces when they were taught that God is the Father of all creatures. I had always known of happiness as some feeling that animals wear as they graze the fields unaware of time or death. Did they know cruelty was close at hand and so lived in a state of...happiness? I did not want to utter the reason for my happiness, lest it should be taken away. I could state candidly in my Diary: *I am happy!*

Summer was approaching and the gables of the house were being cleaned and a few roses had burst their perfume while their petals still held the shape of miniature cabbages. We were eating breakfast when Jason turned to both Graces, and without looking at me, said: 'It's Minor. He's progressing with the words, but is still having delusions that are turning him violent. I am seeking your consent to take Chandreeka with me to Broadmoor to meet him and take safe delivery of his lists of words and quotations. I'm sorry I haven't given much time to any of you for considering this...'

Lady Grace couldn't help herself from smiling and looked at me. 'Chandreeka, what would you like to do?'

'I don't believe I have a choice in the matter Ma'am and it's the first time I've heard of Mr Melville's...'

'Would you choose to go?' she asked again, genuinely interested.

'I believe I still have no choice in the matter Ma'am, Sir, as I'm too far gone the road of collecting words, working our way through the alphabet—how can I resist such an offer—only if it pleases you?'

There was a big sigh of relief. Master Stephen would be with us, as he wanted to visit the Wellington College at Crowthorne.

We had a fortnight to prepare for the journey. I'm not sure why, but I decided to pack the sari in my trunk for good luck. As the travel might interrupt my regular diary, I think it best to write the events of each day as it also might assist in the collation of the quotation slips.

The New World

Stage & Coach Inn, Devonshire, Summer 1873

The journey from King's Lynn was arduous. The train from Paddington to Wellington College Crowthorne railway station was a relief as we watched the scenery dipping and rising past the window, and Master Stephen, Jason and I took short naps. Halts are welcome, but we had so many delays due to flooding on certain roads and changes between coaches that after a while I wondered if we had travelled across land to another country! Master Stephen and I look visibly seasick for want of sea air.

We finally arrived at the Stage and Coach Inn in Crowthorne village. It is a few miles from the Criminal Lunatic Asylum of Broadmoor where Dr W.C. Minor is secured in residence. It is a matter of fascination combined with some horror that Minor, as he is known, was born in Ceylon, had studied to be a medical doctor, was in the American Civil War and had then shot and killed a man when he arrived in Lambeth, London last year.

Horror and fascination best describe the awe I feel on learning of Minor's mental illness and criminal capability. These conditions sit beside his momentous knowledge of words; his skill is renowned in the usage of English language of the sixteenth and seventeenth centuries.

Jason's hard-nosed enquiries along the way, as well as gossip from the coachmen provided evidence about the disturbed disposition of Minor. From all accounts, we've been told it is as if he is many persons seated and standing simultaneously beside his many selves and none of them are aware of the other's presence. He breaks out in violent spells and needs restraining. That is the shock and disturbance, as if he is his own spy and judge. To have so many words, so much language, and yet be powerless to effect understanding or to describe the rupture taking place within. Pity! I survived from my experiences during the horrors of 1857 that severed my roots from everything I had known as my origins. But survival cannot be uniform in people of diverse temperaments and cultures. Perhaps one day the study of the psyche and its labyrinthine ways will be a subject of study and literature by which we can tide over this suffering that we call human.

While Jason left early this morning to collect the post and proceeded to meet Minor, Master Stephen and I had our breakfast at leisure. In fact, we probably were the last to be seated. Stephen's complexion hosting the pallor and speckles of a Siberian Warbler's eggs alarmed the serving girl. She reported it to the kitchen staff. They were determined to give him a dose of glowing health, so we were fed with extra eggs, sausages and bacon to bring some colour into his cheeks. Travel does not suit Stephen well, and I'm afraid Mr Whippet's ambitions for him in the Navy will need serious reconsideration.

Stephen and I decided on a favoured scenic route

for a constitutional walk around the village. Bright red bordered notices for a Magic Act caught my attention. It will be held in an adjacent hall of the Inn where we are staying for several evenings this week and the next. The most striking of all is that it is 'A Hindoo Magician: Raja Coomaradeva—with the Indian Rope Trick'. I am excited and curious and know Stephen will not require much persuasion to accompany me to the Magic Act. Jason might require more convincing. We have ten days here, as Jason will be on his mission of quotation slips, so I'm certain one evening at the Magic Act to see another Indian will be a memorable, if not an eventful, distraction.

I spread out the sari on the bed for good luck. In the candle light the pomegranate-pink silk looked blood red, the sunset orange border blended with the gold; the temple spires were glinting flames on the pallu with Veerappan's name strung like flowers sacrificed at Amman's feet. This sari had travelled from a fibre of his imagination and collided with history. In spite of his abrupt and violent death, the sari had survived and it was my life-line in re-membering my origins.

Whatever language I now speak, think, whatever food I eat with a fork and knife or with my fingers, whatever other names I am called or respond to, I will sail on a rough ocean of Seeraivakkam's silk, laced with the honey of words from different tongues. Just as irony cannot be taught across cultures, I see that lions, boats, fish are symbols, and I know how to unlock their meaning. While I was that girl from Seeraivakkam with only the sari to tell me that truth, I am also the accidental traveller who forged new languages by watching, listening, and constantly learning words—their meanings not always uniform when spoken, written, or thought. That is the life and death distinction between understanding and misunderstanding.

The dark falls on my desk facing the window as I find the time to write in my Diary. I am expecting Stephen with news of tickets to the Magic Act and I can hear footsteps climbing the stairs. There will be a knock any moment, I expect.

11 p.m.

As I was expecting Stephen with news of tickets to the Magic Act, I called out. But to my surprise it was Jason. His face looked relieved, tired and in pain all at once.

He had returned with a bandage around his right hand. 'The man can turn vicious!' he said. Jason was still trembling as if a wild animal had attacked him. 'How can one make sense of how the human mind works? Do you see all these words? The volume of work he has done over the past few months of his being admitted. But he can destroy all that he has created in a flash.

'The Almighty be praised! Thank Goodness you didn't come!' was all he could find the strength to say. I impulsively took his hand and kissed it, and he held my face so close I could see the pain ease into a soulful joy on his face. We stood like that for an eternity, feeling each other's breath on our faces. His hand was bleeding and it was now showing through the gauze bandage.

'Minor…he gave some of the boxes and then got into a fit. I had to restrain him before calling someone. He…bit my hand. It's the effects of the Civil War. He is attacked by memory. He was trained to be a Doctor. He was in charge of branding Deserters. It's too complicated. He lashes out at himself, or at anyone.'

I winced when I heard this. I had experienced human brutality, but unprovoked violence toward a kind and gentle soul seemed unforgivable, in spite of my partiality to Jason. I had not experienced stark raving madness. I gave him some brandy from my hip flask and only Jason could look at it as an interesting object and see the humour in my secrecy.

It was only when he took a swig straight from the flask that I saw his eyes change expression. 'That sari! It…it's travelled all the way from India with you! O my Chandrika! It's all the colour of blood in a sunset!' He ran toward it and felt it. He made me sit on the bed and on his knees as he spoke. 'You are my eternal harvest moon, red with the blood of creation in the sky. I see all the flaming torches of your past, and the light in your soul that carries you into my future. My Chandrika, I have waited all my life for you!'

I was living in a dream.

A good while later, the Doctor arrived with Master Stephen taking charge, and Jason's hand was examined. Stitches and more brandy.

I've had a deep sleep before resuming my diary.

I've managed to compile the quotation slips. Reading the handwriting has become a strain.

I cannot believe nearly a week has passed and so much done and I'm sure there is much more to do. I couldn't continue the journal. I sleep exhaustedly after the walks.

Stephen and I feel it's quite a triumph that we persuaded Jason to come to the Magic Act tonight. I have seen Raja Coomaradeva. His hair is jet black, as are his eyes, which look rather melancholic. But he is very swift in his movements and his wit, even if his English is not entirely fluent.

I am refreshed after dozing off in the chair in the library downstairs. The dream I had was so clear.

It was spring brightening into summer. Jason was at Grace Hall. I walked to St Mary's Church to hand cookies to all the children in the Sunday class with notes of temporary farewell to the older orphan girls. I had a quiet moment in front of the Virgin and placed my life in her hands. I returned early that evening and my sari from Seeraivakkam was spread open like the sky. I was accompanying Jason to America to see a whole new world.

Presences of the Past

Madras, April 1916

Midnight. The grandfather clock sliced the silence in twelve strokes. Jagan and Allarmelu nearly jumped. Dharma was sweating; after reading for five hours, he was hoarse. Allarmelu could see he was clearly absorbed in the history of the sari. Or, was he more fascinated by the writer? She balked at the current of her thoughts of late. Allarmelu released a huge sigh followed by a soft grunt. She was indignant at the abrupt end of the reading. The three of them looked at each other.

Even if Jagan had been unaware of her entering the room, it was no surprise. Quite often, she came in to listen to him reading from Rabindranath Tagore's English translation of *Gitanjali*; a bridge between Literature in English by an Indian Nobel laureate. She couldn't help thinking this was his ploy to get her to read English, with Indian nuances, and by 'eminent men'.

By all means they try to hold me secure who love me
in this world. But it is otherwise with thy love which is
greater than theirs, and thou keepest me free.
Lest I forget them they never venture to leave me alone.
But day passes by after day and thou art not seen.

Stanza 32. Hearing her father read it made her realise that the 'thou' was none other than her mother. Chellamma was the woman he loved beyond all worlds. It was the first time she became aware of her parents as a man and a woman, holding the thread of love in life, and beyond death. A bride's sari was tied to the bridegroom's shawl to signify just that? She often wondered. That love was a secret island she did not have permission to enter and it was independent of her existence.

Dharma blew his nose into a white cotton handkerchief. 'Dharma, you're not going to break down into another tempest, are you?' Jagan said rather distractedly, as he sighed. It was well past his time for settling into bed.

'But I don't understand! Why was all this kept away from me—all these years?' Dharma shut the book and smoothed his hands over its edges.

'I didn't keep anything from you. That day when you brought the European, suddenly it struck me. We never recall our past as history. We think we can remember the same things that others do, and that we live forever. Even if it is a family chronicle, see how important this lady's diary is for us to know why we need to speak, to stand together, call for freedom, as a people? Only now I understand how Chellamma understood things... through that sari.' Jagan spoke with a measured pace as if the profound significance of that sari had finally dawned on him. After a pause, he began humming the melody, from their favourite composer Thyagaraja, that he and Allarmelu had been practising yesterday. He uttered the words so movingly, they needed no accompanying music.

'Nama ruci telusuna?
Do you know the sweet remembrance of That name?
Can the taste of Your name be known to those who are
devoid of Love?
Can the truth about a woman be known to an actor
donning a robe?
Without experiencing happiness, can talking to others
about it bring happiness?
If a terrifying tiger puts on the garb of a cow, would milk
flow from its udder for the calf?

It was enough for Dharma to start slapping his forehead repeatedly and cry out

'Na Tala Raasi! My unmistakable fate!' Allarmelu rushed and held his hands apart knowing the demons he was trying to beat out of himself: stupidity and more stupidity followed by guilt. If she could, she would have beaten them out of him. Jagan stood up; his eyes had an inward gaze and he patted his younger brother's arm, lost in the realisation of a history uncovered. He seemed to have just discovered the breadth of Chellamma's knowledge of the particular and the political. He looked up and began to sing *Telusite Mokhsama.*

Oh no! Not salvation just as yet! Allarmelu thought as she protested against her father's philosophical submerging in saint Annamacharya's lyrics about liberation from worldly desires. She was caught between two men turning away from the real issue and what was at stake. She was faintly aware that her father did not know of the imposter sari. She was vividly aware from Dharma's expression that he was guilty of handing her the imposter. But his remorse was greater at realizing how he was axing down the central pillar of the family's faith by trading that sari for his short-lived and deluded idea of independence.

The flame in the central lamp was spluttering and Jagan walked in a daze toward the oil canister to refill the holder. Allarmelu knew Gowri and Ruku had filled it to its brim before going out with the Governess. It was their gesture of thanks to their eldest brother as he allowed their outings when other patriarchs would have kept women in purdah. They must have returned a while ago and gone silently upstairs from the kitchen so that no questions would be asked about their excursion. How much time must have passed!

Allarmelu could see Dharma's tears beginning a monsoon downpour, with tributaries flowing on to the leather case of Chandrika's diary. She was anxious that it shouldn't smudge the ink. Swiftly and sympathetically she swooped the case away from Dharma who was cradling it as if it was his life contained in one neat box.

Jagan's rendering of Thyagaraja's song saying that the truth about a woman cannot be known by an actor struck both Allarmelu and Dharma in different ways. It refuelled her to avenge the loss of the original sari that Veerappan had woven. It was her last chance to get her father and his brother out of their orbits of self-absorption that were on a collision course. Hmph! And these are men who rule with might over our worlds! She managed to pull herself out of the deluge of dreariness that was settling in the room.

'Naina! How did the sari and this diary come to us, here, all the way from England?'

Jagan could always, even subconsciously, rely on

Allarmelu to revive him from any state of stupor, even death.

'It seems mysterious, but the divine play makes it all possible.'

Allarmelu wanted to stamp her foot when her father spoke in riddles. But she was a 'woman' now, in the room with two muddled men, and she wanted to seem calm and stand her own ground with poise. 'What happened, Naina? I am asking because it was Amma's last wish… the sari's arrival?'

In a voice that was distant yet close, he began the story of the sari's arrival. 'It didn't come to Madras. It went to Tanjavur. Your grandmother Amamma, and Amma always hosted a feast for the pilgrims who gathered at the saint Thyagaraja's festival. The day we heard you were going to be born, both your Amamma and Chellamma started making arrangements for many more gifts as a thanksgiving. Your Amma's father, and his father before him, owned land and the weaver villages around Tanjavur. Amamma commissioned the weavers of Seeraivakkam to spin cloth for the temple deity.

'That day of the festival, your Thatha, Amma's father, gave me sole charge of the land, the weaving villages and that leather case. As he had no son, he gave it to me with tears in his eyes and prayed I would be custodian of what was god's gift to all of us. He mentioned that a certain weaver had come to his father, my Chellamma's grandfather, with this case. That weaver had a son, who loved magical arts and had travelled to Europe with his talents. He brought back with him the sari and the contents in the case.

'How we all rejoiced at the news of your coming! We

didn't read it then. But the first Zamindar mentioned in Chandrika's diary is your Amma's great-great-grandfather. His daughter wanted a sari woven in the Seeraivakkam Amman's name to be handed down the line of mothers and their daughters. As you heard, the divine play had other plans with history, but somehow it came back to us. I always believed that the past has a presence. Sometimes I hear the voice of this Chandrika telling me of what might have happened.'

America, 1879

I have never believed in superstition or magic. So, after being in America nearly four years after leaving England, it seemed strange that Hindu Magician Raja Coomaradeva's neat handwritten note card that I found in my trunk should give light and hope. The meeting had seemed incidental that summer at the Inn. It was the day Stephen and I had returned from our constitutional and we saw the notices. I almost froze when I set eyes on him—Raja Coomaradeva. At the time I thought it was because he was the only other Indian I had seen since my arrival in England. But now, as I picture him, I see his jet black eyes swept up like crescent moons. His jet black hair was parted in the middle and his ear lobes were the size of coat buttons and curved onto his square jawline. It was his gaze—immediate and distant, and then inward.

I did not feel uncomfortable, in fact it was almost comforting as if we knew each other from a very long time ago. I attributed it to us belonging to the same race. He was just behind the red velvet drapes of the small

stage, when Stephen and I walked in, to inquire about
tickets. He must have heard us and suddenly appeared.
The velvet drape with its yellow tassels strung just above
his head made it look like a turban. He was taller than I
expected, for an Indian. He instinctively folded his palms
as Hindus do and his voice was deep and resonant. He
kept looking at my forehead as he said, 'You are most
welcome'. I couldn't help thinking how incorrect his
English was, as we had not thanked him. But now it has
a different meaning.

When Jason, Stephen and I saw his show, with the
continuous ring of applause following every act, small
or extended, his graceful gestures mesmerized us all.
Instead of speaking he used an incantatory tone; incorrect
sentences made sense. After his act, the audience went
into the dining hall of the Inn and animated discussion
began to fill the air. Jason, too, was enthralled and led
me and Stephen to a group who were recounting their
favourite acts and the versatility of Raja Coomaradeva.
It was a humid day, even for England, and as I reached
in my reticule for my fan, I realized I must have dropped
it in the small theatre and went to retrieve it.

When I entered, only the lamps lighting the stage were
on. I made my way to the front row and started searching
around the chairs where we were seated.

'Is this what you are looking for?' It was unmistakably
Coomaradeva's voice.

I turned in the direction of his voice, and there he was,
on stage, holding my lace and bamboo hand fan elegantly.
He held it out to me and as I took it, he held me in his
gaze. The fan became a baton that connected our lives,
as a conductor would make music through an orchestra.

His voice sounded like a bell that balmed the room when he said, 'I, too, come from Seeraivakkam. The past is always present in us. You don't even have to remember it. It flows all around.' As he said this I could see he shifted his gaze from looking into my eyes, to almost reading my forehead. 'You made a long journey. You have more journeys. Nothing is a struggle if you keep travelling. You have met me. Your life…' He took a deep breath.

Just then Stephen called out, not knowing where I was. His back was to the doorway.

'Remember this, I can lift the weight of doom from your soul. Only this matters, that your story must be told.' I broke away from his look of deep concentration and turned toward Stephen. Coomaradeva held out a card and with a voice filled with urgency said, 'We are the clan of Amman's weavers. A life is a story. Ours is told the way it is woven. Anytime, every time, should you need any assistance, I am here, and there', and he handed me his card. His address was impeccably written in India ink:

Raja Coomaradeva *Esq*
Master Magician of the Inner Circle
Patron: Zamindar of Seeraivakkam
Presidency of Madras
INDIA

It all seemed so natural in that moment. As I took his card and put it in my reticule it felt that he read my past and future. How could he have known? I will never know. All I know now is that this story will live on.

To begin, I must revisit the past of these years beginning in America.

The white underside of gulls flying overhead, screeching. The cobalt waves of the sea looked miles away, below us. The ship's deep-bellied horn was blowing in the distance. Hats and dresses were billowing in the cold wind, but the sun and the blue sky with cirrus clouds at midday made for happiness because in my blood and in the air, salt smelt of freedom.

Freedom. That was the journey, or was it a voyage? We had come to see the fossils at Lyme Regis, where Mary Anning had died nearly thirty years ago. She had become lore. Jason wanted to show me the fossils and where the *Icthyosaurus platyodon* had been found before we left the shores of England. I marvelled at the woman's courage to have singlehandedly built a business around her self-taught profession—seeing signs of life in stone.

From the gossip at the inn where we stayed, there were two views about her, both in parliamentary scales of opposition. There were those who had known her since childhood, who verified she died fulfilled, doing what she knew best. The neighbours she had in later life indicated the other view; she died bitter, not getting the recognition she was owed by the British Geological Society. I wondered when women, apart from Queens, would ever get recognition for their discoveries that changed a way of life. What about life itself? Did we need a certificate of completion from an authority?

One view held that she'd had several doses of laudanum to escape her loneliness by getting intoxicated; the other held she'd had a fatal illness (in hushed tones referring to the dreaded cancer of her breast) and took strong doses of laudanum to subdue the pain of the disease which finally killed her. Mary Anning never married, but she knew freedom by the sea, its cliffs, and I couldn't help observing, that for someone who lived on the border of land and sea, she would always have a divided history.

Jason made copious notes from some of the people at Lyme, particularly a certain John Gleed, a Congregational church priest at the church where Mary had been baptized, who had left for the United States of America to campaign for the abolition of slavery. Gleed's departure diminished the number of churchgoers attending the service on Sundays, and Mary switched from being a Congregationalist to becoming an Anglican. I didn't put too much weight on it, but found it curious that one could switch denominations of worship based on the personality of the priest departing and the one who replaced him.

'He must be John-long-gone dead, well before the Civil War. The Thirteenth Amendment is now inscribed in history; why are such good men so few, who would leave their comfort and claim causes on distant lands...' Jason said as he clambered down the pavement to the shore walk that led to the Blue Lias cliffs. 'But John Gleed must be remembered for his valour.' He looked vibrant and it was this quality of Jason's—remembering what others did in the cause of justice—that made my heart swell not solely with admiration, but love.

As we walked under the treacherous cliffs in Mary's path I couldn't help musing on Vishnu and his incarnations. First, he was the fish, then a tortoise, then a land animal; I had been taught as a little girl that it was evolution known as dasavataram, of a time that was without beginning. But when we sat at tea the discussion was often about how the fossils existed for about two thousand years since the recorded history of mankind. Much sense I'd make, talking about my Hindu gods and their ten incarnations! It was the first time I felt I could not share these thoughts with Jason. Perhaps when we went to America, there would be time for me to form the words that spelled the idea.

In spite of the proximity to wars with France, being in the habitat where the fossils were continuously discovered, buyers would come in the name of science to collect, investigate, and in some cases preserve the fossils as trophies, while others would bequeath them to museums to further the exploration of the origins of life.

We went to London. I was overcome at the British Museum. The exhibit of the Icythosauraus was so enormous that I wondered how any child could understand the scale of creatures solely from the drawings Stephen had at our lessons.

The rumbling of the underground railway both in gentlemen's preoccupations and investments, as well as in reality, was a tremendous part of the imagination. I, however, felt it was 'full of sound and fury' signifying steam; a significant waste to me if it was for such a small group of people who could afford it. It would never come to succeed, however ingenious it seemed.

I never thought the moment would arrive. It did. I was aboard SS *The Queen* at Liverpool, where so many voyages of immigrants had taken place. In spite of the age-old traffic of ports, somehow neither the ship, nor the docks nor crew nor passengers looked weary. My eyes were brimming with tears and my heart was full of hope. I had hoped this voyage would be to freedom, my last voyage from seeking, my only voyage to a home of my own, wherever that maybe.

I looked up and the seagulls were swooping and then I felt Jason's reassuring hand around my waist. A porter swiftly came by and doffed his cap and Jason tipped him. I only knew he was a porter because of his deep blue coat and red and gold epaulettes that were embroidered with SS *The Queen*. His manner was exceedingly deferential and I could barely make out his face, for he kept it hidden under the shade of his cap.

We sailed for a few days and my stomach held in good stead. The first time I had cramps, I was so sick, I could feel myself drained of blood. I decided to go and sit on the deck come night or day, just to breathe deeply. I'd look at the stars overhead; some I could decipher and the others looked like such a maze. I wished I could understand them. Why were stories attributed to them? Was light life? Then one night things took a turn.

Jason had gone to the newsroom. The last August daylight was fading. A while later, there was a big commotion, and I heard a solitary crash. The summary of the incident was that Jason had been struck on the head. At the time, I was shocked to see him bandaged and smiling. His eyes as glazed as glass. The porter had not managed to catch the assailant, and the Captain had come to enquire if anything else was needed.

A few nights after that, Jason would scream out in the dark of his cabin, frequently followed by the crash of some object. He would be up to walk with me around the deck the next morning, weary, but endeavouring to be normal. I wondered if that was because of the small dosage of opium he took to keep the pain at bay.

When we arrived in New York, I was taken by the scale of the wide horizon. There was so much to see,

and people to meet, and Jason seemed recovered within
our thirteen-day journey across the Atlantic. He showed
me his office from when he was a reporter for the Civil
War. It had now turned into a trench of shelves carrying
notecards with words collected from the English-
speaking world.

Jason was still on his dictionary trail and wanted to
continue recording words that travelled from distant
ports, and changed through the course of usage during
a voyage along the Atlantic American seaboard. His
curiosity and eager note-taking puzzled me, but in the
evenings when he read things out and made a story of the
day, I heard the sum of parts. I had seen syllables shifting
their shape into words and meanings. The dictionary
collection was his obsession. I continued assisting him
throughout this word programme, sorting English words
that had African, Indian, Arabic, American, Australian
origins. I felt, with the sounds of these words, I had
travelled to all these distant shores.

He continued to take on reporting, apart from
writing pamphlets for different causes. More recently,
his interest was in the Lewis and Clarke expedition
and the Northern territories. He seemed interested in
frontiers, and what would become of the Black Elk and
indigenous inhabitants of the Plains. The Frontier was
a wilderness that was aggressively fought for by white
map-makers. The Indians on the plains had recently
acquired the facility of the horse, so were not as nomadic
as the Indians further south. Jason had done a feature on
horses being slaughtered following the Civil War. 'They
find it too radical. My report on the horse…they seem to
think it shows me criticizing the Government and siding
with the Indians.'

One day Jason came in and said, 'I have a new lead on the trail of a murder.'

'Is this recent?' I asked

'Oh no! I'm interested because it's a tale of greed and loss… Er… how would you feel if we were to move for a little while?'

I must have been at that time of the month, and it was freezing that November. My fingers had been bleeding out of dryness and were ink stained. I still lived alone and was working toward the great project, but there weren't enough coals to stoke the fire. I looked up and my eyes must have flashed. He knew what I was thinking.

'We could get married and live together under one roof when we get to Bozeman.'

'Why not here?'

'Only because I've been called to relook at some recent evidence on the founder of Bozeman. John Bozeman, it is believed, may not have been killed; he could've been murdered by his partner.'

It was freezing in New York and I was now being told we had to move to the north, bordering Canada. I felt chained to a belief that was beginning to reveal itself as a decoy for something else. Only, I couldn't make out what it was. I was afraid my doubt would become transparent. I had nowhere to turn to, as all my letters to Lord and Lady Grace were being returned undelivered. I would see letters opened and returned to their envelopes on Jason's desk in his study. It was apparent there was a steady loss in his investments and his finances were dwindling. I worked without pay, and now offered my assistance in a haberdashery over the weekend to get some real money for food. I was weary of being viewed as chattel, in spite of being met by gentlemen and ladies who engaged me in conversation about literature and colonial affairs. When I wrote, it was under a pseudonym and the payment by cheque was always in Jason's name. This may not have been qualified as slavery, but the experience enslaved my being as I had ventured out on love and trust.

'What's the profit in going all the way to Bozeman?' I said as calmly as I could, trying to control the tears of hunger and wretchedness that were going to overcome my studied composure.

'Damn you!' He hurled the empty glass lamp at me. 'Do you know how much I'm suffering?'

This was like the many rows we had over the last few months. I had seen the same porter from SS *The Queen* appear at frequent intervals to deliver parcels when the ship arrived at port. At first I thought they were bundles of word notes from the colonies. But wedged within those were parcels of opium that Jason consumed. He was now ordering batches for sale. How could I get away from this? Why don't dreams signpost nightmares?

As I took the dustpan and began sweeping the shards of broken glass from the threadbare carpet, my hunger and fatigue gave me a new weapon. Cunning. I decided to save the money from the haberdashery and also go with Jason to Montana, believing he would marry me. It would give me legitimacy to continue living in America. This was the New World, and I was determined to free myself at any cost.

I was aware he would give either very short notice or none at all for appointments or the reports that I was writing, so I decided to be packed and ready. Starvation and prostitution were the only doorways open, it seemed. I was a survivor of the Mutiny; this was too easy.

I kept my 'Globetrotter Trunk' well-hidden and secured. When I knew he would be out for the day I cranked open the lid. There was the ivory Chantilly-lace stole that Lady Grace gave me as a parting gift. When she had placed it in my hands, she had looked at me, her grey-blue eyes widening as she wished me a deep and genuine draught of happiness. My eyes welled then, as they do now. I knew that the Graces had no inkling of this other side to Jason, which had taken over him. I wanted to hide the stole, so that Jason in his inexplicable rantings wouldn't throw it into the fire. He seemed to rage without cause at any recollection of mine from my past at Grace Hall. Stephen and Isobel's names were forever silenced.

The trunk had a false bottom, and I had concealed the cash from my haberdashery earnings there. When I removed it, there was the silk sari, all the way from Seeraivakkam, with my name in Tamil rippling across its body. I wondered at the voyage of this sari—an original commission of Veerappan, from silk saved by the Zamindar—a labour of love. From it, Raja Coomaradeva's card slipped out. Suddenly, the thought of Seeraivakkam, Amman, and Kali as the force of time, flashed. I trembled with fear and then with hope. I am now packing the sari into a cushion with this leather case that contains my life and couriering it to Raja Coomaradeva. I pray it reaches him.

A Woman

After lunch the next day, when everyone was having a nap, Allarmelu had invited an unlikely guest. She held out a stainless steel tumbler of steaming, sweet tea and a hot-cross bun that had just been delivered from Puraswalkam's Whitefield bakery.

'Kuppu, you know what I know. So, where is the sari?'

'Amma, Amma, what are you saying Amma! How will I know the things of such a great household?' Kuppu went into deferential mode, while protesting against any allegation of conspiracy. Allarmelu accepted the power he placed in her, while mentally acknowledging her father for the high status she had been given since he became a widower. He could have placed the power in his sisters, her aunts, but invested it in her instead.

'Your brother, Perumal, told me you know the weaver who darns very well. He was watering the red hibiscus plant this morning, and offered the flowers for prayers at the shrine, while placing the sacred cross on himself. Your brother couldn't be telling us lies?'

'Aiyiyo! No Amma! He never tells what is not true.' A pause. Then, 'Your Chinnaina, very good man.'

'I know my Chinanina is a honourable and good man.

And I believe he knows what is best, for him. That's why he trusts you, and pays you for your work. That gives you a good living, doesn't it?' Allarmelu could see through Kuppu. Years of hardship had made him immune to praise or blame. But she had managed to win him over and she knew it was because she had a purpose.

Kuppu decided to unravel what he knew. 'I warning Sir, "be careful, be careful". He no listening. Simply making plans. He promising Beppo Sir Tanjavur silk for Russian dance drama, and money.'

On hearing the word 'money,' Allarmelu's stomach lurched. Where on earth did her delightful and decadent Uncle think the money was coming from other than her father and *Surya Vilas*?

'Kuppu, my mother, Periamma sent a sari through Sir to be repaired. That was nearly four years ago… The sari that came back to *Surya Vilas* is not the same one. Who was the weaver who repaired it?' Allarmelu had to stop her voice from breaking.

'Aiyiyo! Amma, that sari was never handed to the weaver for repair!'

Kuppu's revelation in the kitchen had set Allarmelu's thoughts into a cyclone. If Chinnaina didn't give the sari that Amma had given him on the day of the picnic for repair, why was he keeping it? Then again, if as Kuppu said, he never gave the sari to the weaver, why did Dharma Chinnaina promise Amma that she would be able to wear it after it was repaired, for Pongal? Was it stolen, or had he stooped so low and sold the sari?

On the eleventh day of the waxing moon, Allarmelu

told her aunts that she wanted to go to the family Amman temple at Barnabas Road to remember her mother and perform the rites; this time, however, she wanted to go there alone.

It was 2:30 in the afternoon. She sat in the carriage, and as it wheeled out of the driveway, she swiftly put a burqa on. The coachman knew he was on a special mission. Instead of turning on to Barnabas Road, he speeded toward Kelly's Road. Kuppu was waiting by the Oteri canal bridge. He seemed to know the way. The carriage stopped at a building washed in yellow ochre with a bottle-green signpost: THE RAILWAY HOTEL ANNEXE.

The stairwell was wooden with coir carpeting, which still smelled of dried fish, and wet dog fur. The ground floor was unattended. These were private apartments, with quiet corridors.

One room upstairs had the door slightly ajar. Allarmelu heard a foreigner's voice. 'Well, what do you think?' Allarmelu peered through the slender opening of the door. Valentina was standing on the bed in a lacy satin chemise, with the pomegranate-pink sari draped along her right shoulder.

'Valentina! What are you doing?'

Allarmelu gulped; nothing could loosen that knot in her stomach or the pounding in her chest when she recognized her Chinaina Dharma's voice. She stood by the side of the doorway concealed in the shadow and her burqa.

'Let's pretend we are married, shall we?' Valentina teased.

'You can't! Take that off right now!'

'Well, if we can't make love, then we must use it for

the costume...' She had moved close to the window, and now held the sari out, away from her, as if inviting him to catch it.

'Nothing of the sort! You hear me? The drama stops now.' Dharma was threatening.

'*Drama?* Who is the one who is play-acting all the time? You followed me to Europe. You think you can have a baby from that woman, and two mistresses, and just walk away? When we met years ago, our world had turned, you even dropped this sari because you found me.'

'Valentina! You're playing with fire. Just give it to me.'

'Beppo knows, and it is decided that I must return with him. Come to me, it'll be our last time.'

'Can you not understand? I've seen what happens at war in Europe. It's still not ended. I came back alive. I will never be free until I return this sari. Listen to me, whatever we do, just leave that sari alone and give it back to me!' Dharma was pleading.

Allarmelu felt an indefinable force urging her to act. In her burqa, she dashed into the room and jumped on the bed, pulling the bundled sari away from Valentina, who was standing by the headboard. Dharma was reeling at the far end of the room, holding his head in his hands. Allarmelu pulled up her burqa and stuffed the sari into a bag she was carrying under it. A shot was fired in the courtyard below. Dharma shouted and fled through the bathroom and the fire escape. As Allarmelu turned to watch, Valentina hurled herself from the window.

Down below, hidden out of range from the balcony, Allarmelu saw Beppo, carrying a Winchester rifle, with Lali, who was sitting in an open cart filled with mangoes. Four men laid out a large sheet and caught the free-falling

Valentina. They wrapped her as she struggled to get free, suppressed her screams, and bundled her into the back of the cart. Dharma was still thumping down the iron spiral stairs to get to the courtyard.

As Dharma turned into the courtyard, Beppo screamed words that rang like bullets in a language she knew was not English. The last Allarmelu saw of Beppo was a very red face, and white fingers clutching the rifle, as the cart swerved. He cried out, 'It's over!'

Allarmelu heard her uncle sobbing by the corner of the brick wall facing the courtyard, mumbling, 'It's over' again and again.

The sari was safely hidden in the bag on her belly. She held on to it, walking out of the Railway Annexe dignifiedly, like a pregnant woman. The original sari was hers now. Kuppu opened the carriage door. The coachman, none other than Perumal Joseph, drove quietly. Kuppu parted the crowds.

Surya Vilas, July 1916

Allarmelu was dressed as a bride and her father did not stint on the musicians and dancers for the katcheri, nor her headdress and jewellery. Kanna dressed Allarmelu, who liked the way the headdress parted her hair in the centre. Kanna reminded her of the rhymes they made up about the hemispheres. The crescent moon worn in the left 'hemisphere' of her head, and the sun on the right. They were the size of small pappadums. The sun, rubies and diamonds in the centre, was encircled with rows of pearls. The moon was a crescent, also bordered with pearls, but filled with emeralds and rubies, with one large central diamond. Her eyes were lined with kartikai, her soft downy eyebrows were shaped as arcs. *Every step forward from the past marks my future*, she told herself. The necklaces and pendants her mother wore glinted around her neck and torso.

Lali was commissioned to sing and there were whispers among more orthodox guests about the shocking liberality of *Surya Vilas*, that a 'mistress' of one of the members of the family should be paraded in a private family rite. But Allarmelu had insisted that Lali sing the conventional programme of invocations to Ganesha (and he *had* removed obstacles), devotional, and love songs. Lali's six-year-old, Chellamma, was also there. It reassured Allarmelu of her mother's incarnation in this life-changing ceremony.

Dharma was there. Men, only older and close relatives of the family were allowed to attend. Allarmelu looked at him. He had regained the light in his face and was conspicuously sociable with guests. The ceremony had tiers of guests. There were relatives across generations that included second and third cousins from Tanjavur, Nacharguddi, Kumbakonnam, Pondicherry, Cuddalore and Madras. Weavers from Seeraivakkam were sitting in the courtyard to take part in the ritual.

Dharma was talking to friends who might know of prospective bridegrooms to make a good match for Allarmelu. Allarmelu watched the way he did not even cast a glance of recognition, or acknowledgement at Lali, her singing or her presence. Or even at his little daughter, Chellamma, in public. She knew that was how 'it was done.'

Then there were Jagan's close friends, who had known Allarmelu since she was born. The Governesses were there too, as this was a debut. Allarmelu was not being presented to royalty, or for that matter, to any particular person; the ceremony was an acknowledgement of her sexuality, to the gods and their priests. It was also an awakening of social status. Now she was properly considered the 'lady of the house' as she would have to 'preside' at rituals and ceremonies, and stay within the women's enclosure on days when her menstrual cycle began.

Kanna sat beside her at the ceremony, ensuring all the silver and gold vessels were filled with milk, honey, turmeric, sandalwood paste, vermillion, betel-nut leaves. The yellow mountain plantains were arranged in dozens, like women's open hands. On silver trays there were double strings of jasmine, rice, jaggery, ghee lamps. Little silver bowls were filled with water fragranced with tulasi and sarsaparilla. All these were placed beneath the Tanjavur image of Amman; the altar celebrating fertility and fecundity, along with the real sari, unrepaired.

Allarmelu beamed with satisfaction as she glanced at her mother's sari, woven with a hidden history, edged with the weaver S. Veerappan's signature. The tassels spilling out in copper and gold sat folded in nine yards of pomegranate pink silk. The body had ripples of *chandrikachandrikachandrika* peeping out at the ceremony, which announced that now Allarmelu was an embodiment of Amman, preceded by many mothers and their daughters, a woman.

Glossary

**D. = Deccani; H. = Hindustani; S. = Sanskrit;
T.= Tamil; Te. = Telugu;**

- Aadi (T., Te.)   mid-year in the Tamil calendar, hot season, July-August

- Aiya (T.)   Lit. 'father'; a respectful suffix, used as an honourific

- Akka (T., Te.)   Older sister, an elder woman

- Annamacharya   Tallapaka Annamacharya, composer and poet of Carnatic music (1408-1503 CE)

- Anni (T.)   Wife of an elder brother; sister-in-law

- Almira (H.)   Cupboard

- Ayah (H.)   Nanny

- Badaam (H.)   Almond

- Bandicoot/ Pandikokka (Te.)   Large burrowing rodent, lit. 'pig rat', as it destroys crops in fields

- Bangaru (Te.)   Lit. 'golden one'; an endearment

- Carnatic   South Indian system of classical music

- Che che   Noises expressing mock exasperation

- Chandrika (S.)   Ray of the moon

- Chatram (T.)   palmyra roofing

- Chinnaina (Te.)   Lit. 'younger father', used for uncles and close older males

- Chola   South Indian dynasty c. 300-1279 CE; also bronze sculptures from that dynasty

- Coromandel Coast   South eastern coast of India, spanning today's Andhra Pradesh and Tamil Nadu, along the Bay of Bengal. It was named by the Portuguese, who got the name from Cholamandalam, or the 'realm of the Chola'.

- Deccani/Dakhani   Dialect spoken in Hyderabad, S. India, that mixes Urdu with Telegu, Marathi, Kannada, Arabic, Turkish and Persian, as the area formed the southern boundary of the Mughal Empire.

- Dhara (S.)   Thread, in this case

- Dhoti (H.)   Indian gentleman's attire, cloth folded from waist to ankle

- Docgaru (Te.)   Doctor+garu; respectful suffix in Telegu

- Fiteel (T.)   Carnatic violin; acculturation of 'fiddle'

- Gajjarasi (T.)   A breed of rice cultivated in Tanjavur

- Ganga   The most sacred river for Hindus; water taken from the river is sprinkled as symbolic purification for diverse rites of passage.

- Gup shup (H., D.)   Gossip, chit-chat

- Halwa (H.)   Sweet made from semolina

- Homa (S.)   Fire-ritual

- Idli (T.)   Steamed rice dumpling, native to South India

- *Iramavtaram*   Tamil *Ramayanam*, composed by Kampan (c.1180-1250 CE)

- Jaggery   Cane sugar concentrated into a solid mass

- Jagruti (T.)   Beware

- Jubba (Te.)   South Indian man's shirt with tails

- Kadamba (T.)   Sweet-smelling flowers of the *Neolamarckia cadamba* tree

- Kaliyuga (S.)   Lit. 'Age of Iron'; signifies the decline of the world into materialism when used colloquially, particularly in Tamil and Telugu.

- Kanjeevaram (Kanchipuram)   A temple town; the style of silk sari woven there

- Kannagi   A legendary woman; central character of the Tamil epic *Silapathikaram* (c. 100-300 CE), who challenged the Pandyan King at Madurai for the murder of her husband; she is iconic for her chastity and rage against injustice.

- Kannakambaram (T.)   Orange flower used in garlands for temple offerings and women's hair

- Kapathu (T.)   Seeking protection

- Kartikai (T., Te.)   Kohl for eyes, made from carbonized ghee

- Khus, roja (H.)   Vetiver, rose attar: Indian perfumes

- Kurathai   From the Kuravar community; hunters, gatherers, trades and crafts people, now migrants.

- Kuruvanji   Ethnic Tamil group from a mountainous region of southern India; mentioned in Sangam literature c. 11 CE. They are also tribal gypsies, and were placed under the Criminal Tribes Act, 1871 by the British and kept very low in the social scale (*cf.* film by Dakxinkumar Bajrange: *Birth 1871, State and Arts of Denotified Tribes of India.*)

- Laddu (H.)   A spherical confectionary encrusted with nuts

- Mariamman (T.)   Aspects of Shakti as Amman

- Moda (H.)   Portable jute stool

- Multani mitti (H.)   Face pack made with clay from Multan, a region in Punjab, today in Pakistan.

- Murku (T.)   A savoury rice pretzel, common snack in South India

- Naina (Te.)   Father

- Nandri (T.)   Thank you

- Nataraja   Shiva in cosmic dance, overcoming delusion

- Noolkol (Te.)   Root vegetable used in korma

- Paan (H.)   Betel-leaf rolled with condiments

- Pallu (H.)   The free end of the sari that is displayed

- Pandal (S.)   Marquee tied to pillars, open on all sides

- Pannade (T.)   Uncouth

- Pariah (Te.)   Lit. someone or something that is outside the recognized parameters

- Parijata (T.)   Night-blooming jasmine, the flowers of which are offered to Krishna

- Parthasarathi   Krishna, as an avatar of Vishnu, acting as soul's guardian and the charioteer of Arjuna in the *Mahabharata.*

- Pavadai (T. Te.)   Ankle-length skirt worn by girls

- Paya (D.)   Goat's trotters cooked in a curry

- Periamma (T.)   Aunt on the mother's side of the family

- Pice (H.)   British Indian coin; currency from the colonial era

- Pista (D.)   Pistachio nut, the fruit of the *Pistacia vera* tree

- Pondatee (T.)   Wife

- Pongal (T.)   Harvest, new

- Purandara Dasa   Telegu poet and composer (1484-1564)

- Rasam (T.)   A soup made from tamarind, served with rice as a digestive

- Rudraksh (S.)   Lit. 'Rudra's tears', from when He was overwhelmed while contemplating satchitananda: existence-knowledge-bliss. The name of a tree, *Elaeocarpus Ganitrus Roxb*, the seeds of which are considered holy and used in rosaries for meditation

- *Sakuntala*   Sanskrit drama by Kalidasa c. 500 CE

- Samrani (Te.)   Indian frankincense

- Shabaash (H., D.)   An accolade

- Shahi-tukda (D.)   Hyderabadi dessert

- Sokai (T.)   A tunic top or blouse, usually worn with a pavadai by girls

- Sumangali (Te.)   A married woman, who has not been widowed

- Surya Vilas   Lit. the house of the sun

- Sutra (S.)   'Threads' of discourse, set out in aphorisms, containing a doctrine in Hindu law and philosophy

- Sutradhara (S.)   The Storyteller or the one who holds the narrative thread in theatre

- Talam (T.)   The classification of beats in Carnatic music

- Tanjore (Tanjavur)   Temple town; its eponymous style of painting

- Tanboora (Tanpura)   A string instrument to keep pitch

- Teepoy (T.)   Small table, used for tea, usually with three legs

- Tennikoit   Tennis played with rubber rings; popular on cruise ships in the early twentieth century

- Tholabommalattu (Te.) Leather shadow puppets

- Thyagaraja   Carnatic music composer (1767-1847 CE)

- Tonga (H.)   Pony-drawn public coach

- Tulasi   Indian basil; worshipped as a deity in houses and temples; the leaves are also used an insect repellent

- Upumau (Te.)   South Indian tiffin savoury, made from semolina

- Veena (S.)   String instrument with double base gourds characteristic of Carnatic music

- Zamindar (H.)   Landlord

Acknowledgements

In the constellation of inspiration, I am fondly indebted to Usha Aroor who pulled me out of the trenches. To the kestrel eyes of Jim Crace, Louise Doughty, and Ravi Singh, for their close reading and making this novel happen. Dr Darryll Grantley for urging this got written; Dr Nina Taunton for her observations; Michael Lopatagui who aligned differences to make it coherent. To Rukhsana Ahmad for seeing the familiar in the unfamiliar and shared diasporicities; to Evalyn Lee and her insights on migrations in a century of silk. To Professor Francesca Orsini of SOAS for understanding serendipity, Storytellers and local oral literatures. To Professor Huw Bowen for the Legatum Institute lecture on *Making Money, Making Empires: The Case of the East India Company*. To Dr Hanne M deBruin and Rajagopal for Kanchipuram's Kaikkolar and Kattaikuttu. To Dr Suresh Kumar and the Dravidian sensibility when Sanskirt was taking over, as well as Tamil translations; and to Vani Vasudevan for spellings in Tamil.

The British Library and The London Library for furnishing me with documents and the geniality that comes from resourceful librarians, and Dr Mukulika Banerjee for the first reading.

Thanks to Mita Kapur of Siyahi for her no-nonsense depth and support; Shalini Krishan, my editor, for alerting me to the difference between discourse and fiction.

To an ocean of family—Arundhati Menon and the spirit of the symbolism in sari, Hari, Viji, Mala, Calpakkam cousins, Shibani, and nephews for recounting the laughter of Madras gone by. To Jackie and Stephen Newbould for sound sense.

To Lakshmi Holmstrom who read, wrote by hand the names of Chandrika and Veerappan in Tamil the very last time I saw her, and who was ever my southern compass. To Girish Karnad for bridging Theatre and the southern story. To Judith Weir for the shape of sound and her deep listening of Storytelling.

To Solerikadu, Nemmelli, Chengalpattu villages and the OrumathAmman koil and its inhabitants for their participation.

To Swami Tripurananda for discussions on modifications, relativity, and the constant. To Chris, who has waited far too long, held faith in my writing, only hell and heaven know why, dared to voyage the turbulence of unspoken colonial histories with me AND put hot food on my plate in very dire times with love—eternal thanks.